DIASPORA PROPERTY FORMULA™

Your Trusted System for Safe Property Investment in Nigeria — From Anywhere in the World

Abiodun D. Doherty

Copyright © 2025 Abiodun D. Doherty

First Edition 2025

ISBN: 978-1-7643149-0-9 (epub)

ISBN: 978-1-7643149-1-6 (paperback)

Published by: Abiodun Doherty

A catalogue record for this book is available from the National Library of Australia

For more information about Abiodun D. Doherty, speaking engagements, seminars, or media interviews, please visit:

www.diasporapropertyformula.com

Printed in Australia

DEDICATION

To every Nigerian in the diaspora who dreams of owning a piece of home—this book is for you. Your sacrifices in foreign lands deserve to translate into lasting wealth and deep connection to your heritage.

To my family, whose unwavering love and support have been my anchor through every challenge and triumph.

To those who have been misled, disappointed, or defrauded in their property journey—may this book be your pathway to redemption, confidence, and the success you deserve.

To the countless professionals in Nigeria who work with integrity to serve diaspora investors—thank you for making dreams possible and proving that trustworthy partnerships can bridge any distance.

And to the Almighty God, who turns dreams into reality and makes all things possible

PRAISE FOR DIASPORA PROPERTY FORMULA

"Having had the privilege of hosting Abiodun Doherty as a guest lecturer at Lagos Business School, I have witnessed firsthand his ability to translate complex legal and investment concepts into practical strategies that resonate with business professionals. His 'Diaspora Property Formula' demonstrates the same analytical rigor and systematic approach that impressed our faculty and students during his presentations. As an educator who has observed Nigeria's evolving investment landscape for decades, I recognize the critical gap that exists between diaspora capital and productive domestic investment opportunities. Abiodun's dual legal expertise in Nigerian and international property law, combined with proven market experience, provides diaspora investors with a framework that balances opportunity with essential risk management. This book represents a significant contribution to bridging the knowledge gap that has prevented many qualified diaspora professionals from participating meaningfully in Nigeria's property market growth.

Professor Olawale Ajai, Lagos Business School

Professor of the Legal, Social and Political Environment of Business and Head, Department of Strategy and Entrepreneurship.

Diaspora Property Formula is a timely and much-needed guide for Nigerians in the diaspora who aspire to invest back home with confidence and clarity. Abiodun Doherty brings over 25 years of legal practice and real estate expertise, offering a credible, tested, and practical roadmap that eliminates the risks that have held many back. This book fills a crucial gap in the market by transforming property investment from speculation into a systematic wealth-building strategy, making it an indispensable resource for anyone serious about creating lasting value in Nigerian real estate.

Abidemi Olugbenga Akinloye, Executive Director, RIM Consulting South Australia

The Diaspora Property Formula has truly transformed my approach to investing. As someone living abroad, I now have a clear grasp of the essential actions needed to steer clear of expensive errors. Abiodun's advice is not only practical and proven but also incredibly motivating. I highly recommend this book to anyone looking to invest wisely and confidently.

Jay Ochuko Adasen, Engineer, Adelaide, Australia

"For too long, Nigerians abroad have faced uncertainty and risk when investing back home. Drawing on deep expertise in the property market, this book brings clarity and practical guidance. Diaspora

Property Formular is exactly the guide our community has needed, empowering diasporans to turn opportunity into lasting wealth in Nigeria."

Emmanuel Ijezie, President, Nigerian Association in South Australia

Diaspora Property Formula is a timely and essential guide for Nigerians abroad who want to invest back home with confidence. Abiodun Doherty distills over two decades of legal and real estate expertise into a clear, practical system that removes uncertainty and protects investors from costly mistakes. This book fills a critical gap in the market by offering both strategic insight and practical tools, making it an indispensable resource for diasporans seeking to turn property investment in Nigeria into lasting wealth.

Damilola Oyeyinka, Founder & Director D Great group Pty Ltd, Adelaide, Australia

This book is a gold-mine for all financially empowered Nigerians in diaspora. As a person who have lived abroad for over 20 years, the mastery knowledge and practical techniques in this book will positively expose Nigerians in diaspora to rare investment opportunities to safely multiply their present wealth. Abiodun is a close friend of over three decades, known for trustworthiness, diligence, excellence and wealth management. I wholeheartedly recommend this book as one of the best on this subject.

- Engr. Tunde Aina P.Eng. PMP, British Columbia, Canada

As a seasoned professional in the practice area of real estate law, I am delighted to introduce Abiodun Doherty's latest book, Diaspora Property Formula. With well over 30 years of experience and a deep understanding of the market, Abiodun Doherty provides invaluable insights and expert guidance for navigating the complex world of real estate in Nigeria. This comprehensive guide offers practical advice, actionable strategies, and expert analysis, making it an indispensable resource for anyone looking to succeed in the industry. Whether you are a seasoned investor, a first-time homebuyer, or a real estate professional, Diaspora Property Formula is a must-read. Abiodun Doherty has done an outstanding job of distilling his knowledge and expertise into a clear, concise, and engaging narrative. The book is filled with real-world examples, case studies, and best practices that will help readers avoid common pitfalls and achieve their goals. I highly recommend Diaspora Property Formula to anyone seeking to gain a deeper understanding of the Nigerian real estate market and stay ahead of the curve. Abiodun Doherty has made a significant contribution to the field, and I am honored to endorse his work.

Nicholas O Omere, Principal Counsel

Law Office of Nicholas O Omere

Solicitor & Advocate of the Supreme Court of Nigeria;

Solicitor & Advocate of the Law Society of Upper Canada.

Abiodun delivers with such clarity and authenticity that it finally brings the peace of mind investors have long been seeking in real estate investments. The Diaspora Property Formula is an invaluable guide filled with deep insights, practical knowledge, and genuine transparency.

Atinuke Kudaisi, Managing Partner, Primrose Law Office, Lagos, Nigeria .

Diaspora Property Formula is an essential guide for Nigerians abroad seeking to invest confidently in property back home. Authored by a seasoned legal practitioner, real estate columnist for The Punch Newspaper, and guest lecturer at Lagos Business School, the book offers unmatched expertise and credibility. It addresses common diaspora concerns—fraud, unreliable contractors, and legal ambiguity—with clear, actionable strategies. Readers are equipped to build, buy, or invest with legal assurance and cultural insight. This book is a trusted blueprint for turning distant dreams into secure, lasting assets.

Toyin Giwa, Clinical nurse and Casual Register, Flinders University, Adelaide, Australia.

I am delighted to endorse Mr Abio dun for his unparalleled business acumen and deep commercial insight into Nigeria's dynamic property market, where he has consistently executed medium to large volume transactions with precision and integrity. His extensive experience—spanning 25 years of successful investments, a respected columnist at The Punch, and guest lecturing at Lagos Business School—makes him uniquely qualified to guide diaspora Nigerians through the complexities of remote real estate investing. This book addresses a glaring void in the market by delivering a systematic, risk based approach that empowers the diaspora to convert their foreign earnings into secure, high return property assets back home. In doing so, it not only bridges the information gap but also unlocks a powerful engine for wealth creation and economic development across Nigeria.

Mr Abimbola Odeyinde, Enterprise Architect Manager, United Kingdom.

"As an entrepreneur who understands the challenges of building wealth across borders, I recognize the value of Abiodun Doherty's systematic approach to Nigerian property investment. The Diaspora Property Formula provides the legal framework and risk management strategies that diaspora investors need to participate confidently in Nigeria's growing real estate market."

Samuel Harrison, Entrepreneur, USA

"Living in Scotland while maintaining strong ties to Nigeria, I understand the unique challenges diaspora investors face when trying to build wealth back home. Abiodun Doherty's Diaspora Property Formula addresses these challenges with the professional expertise and systematic approach that transforms property investment from speculation into strategic wealth building."

Ibukun Aderibigbe, Scotland

" As someone based in London, I understand the challenges diaspora Nigerians face when trying to invest back home. That's why Abiodun Doherty's Diaspora Property Formula stands out - it combines trusted legal guidance with a clear, strategic system that makes property investment in Nigeria not only possible, but profitable and secure. It's the confidence every diaspora investor needs to build lasting wealth from abroad.."

Adetokunbo Rosiji, London

The author of the book "Diaspora Property Formula" is vastly experienced and understand the nuances of acquiring property in Nigeria. On a personal note, the author provided me guidance that opened my eyes to the risks involved in purchasing property while residing abroad. I strongly recommend this book as a trusted guide for anyone in the diaspora looking to avoid pitfalls and make informed decisions to purchase property in Nigeria –

Henry Dukeh, Global Lead, IT Risk Management, Houston, USA

"Operating businesses across multiple markets has taught me the critical importance of having systematic, legally sound investment strategies. Abiodun Doherty's Diaspora Property Formula provides exactly this for Nigerian real estate—a comprehensive system that eliminates guesswork and reduces risk while capitalizing on one of Africa's most dynamic property markets."

Thomas Akagbosu, Chicago, USA

As Nigeria's Acting High Commissioner to Australia, I am delighted to endorse Abiodun Doherty's upcoming book on diaspora investments in real estate in Nigeria. This comprehensive guide provides valuable insights and practical advice for investors looking to tap into Nigeria's growing real estate market.

The book highlights the opportunities and challenges of investing in Nigeria's real estate sector, offering a nuanced understanding of the market trends, regulatory framework, and investment strategies.

I highly recommend this book to anyone interested in exploring the vast potential of Nigeria's real estate market. Abiodun Doherty has done an excellent job in shedding light on this critical area of investment, and I have no doubt that this book will become a go-to resource for investors and stakeholders alike.

Congratulations to Abiodun Doherty on this impressive work. I look forward to seeing the impact it will have on promoting diaspora investments in Nigeria's real estate sector.

Ambassador Dr.Jane Adams
Acting High Commissioner of Nigeria to Australia, accredited to
New Zealand, Fiji, Papua New Guinea, Vanuatu, Tonga, Samoa,
Solomon Islands and Nauru.

FOREWORD

I served between 1980 and 2015 (approximately three decades) in the Nigerian Foreign Service as a Career Diplomat. I worked in major capitals of the world such as Brussels, New York (twice), Tel Aviv, Israel; Nairobi, Kenya; and Vienna, Austria. Eventually, I was appointed as Ambassador and posted to Australia as High Commissioner of Nigeria with concurrent accreditation to New Zealand, Fiji, Papua New Guinea, and Vanuatu.

In all these locations, I met Nigerians who were eager to buy and own property or a number of properties in their beloved home, Nigeria. This was either for personal reasons or as an investment in anticipation of when they return home, or an investment for returns when they retire. In their quest for this laudable initiative by Nigerians in the Diaspora, many have fallen into the wrong hands of fake real estate developers. Many have lost money to these so-called real estate developers. In some cases, they lose money to relatives who are supposed to be developing properties for them. Usually, when they lose money, they come to the Embassy for assistance, there is little the embassy can do.

That is why I commend Lawyer Doherty for writing this book designed to guide Nigerians in the Diaspora in their quest to own property or invest at home.

The numbers tell a compelling story. Our diaspora community sends over $25 billion home annually—a reflection of the enduring love for Nigeria and our families. Yet less than five percent of these resources find their way into the real estate investment sector. The gap between desire and action has persisted not from lack of capital or commitment, but from the absence of a trusted, systematic approach to navigating the complexities of cross-border property investment.

This is why Abiodun Doherty's "Diaspora Property Formula" is coming at an appropriate time when the government is encouraging the Nigerian Diaspora to be part of the goal of making Nigeria a $1 trillion economy by 2030.

The work of Lawyer Abiodun Doherty is groundbreaking, and what distinguishes this book from the countless property investment guides available today is its author's unique knowledge at the intersection of legal expertise, international experience, and deep cultural understanding.

I commend this book to members of the Nigerian Diaspora across the world and even Nigerians at home.

Ambassador Ayoola Olukanni

Former Nigerian High Commissioner to Australia with concurrent accreditation to New Zealand, Fiji, Papua New Guinea and Vanuatu

Former Director General, Nigerian Association of Chambers of Commerce, Industry, Mines and Agriculture (NACCIMA)

ABOUT THE AUTHOR

Abiodun D. Doherty is a seasoned legal practitioner, real estate strategist, and trusted voice on diaspora property investment, with over two decades of experience across Nigeria and Australia. He is the Principal Partner of Abiodun D. Doherty & Co., a respected Lagos-based law firm specializing in property law, and the Director of De Kings Global Trading & Services Pty Ltd, which connects Nigerians in the diaspora with education and strategic investment opportunities.With a unique blend of legal expertise and real-world investment insight, Abiodun has helped hundreds of diaspora clients avoid costly mistakes and invest safely in Nigeria's real estate market. His reputation for integrity, due diligence, and results has made him a go-to advisor in a sector often fraught with fraud and misinformation.

Abiodun has led seminars, coaching programs, and community workshops across major diaspora hubs, empowering Nigerians abroad to build wealth and legacy through smart property investments. His expert insights have been featured in leading Nigerian media, including The Punch, and he is a frequent speaker at conferences and forums focused on diaspora engagement and wealth creation.He holds a Master of Laws (LL.M.) from the University of Lagos, with specialization in Company, Commercial, and Property Law, and is also a licensed Australian Realtor—giving him rare cross-border expertise in international property transactions.

Whether you're a first-time buyer or a seasoned investor, Abiodun's mission is simple: to help you invest back home, confidently and securely.

TABLE OF CONTENTS

PREFACE

For years, I've listened to the concerns of hardworking Nigerians in the diaspora—nurses, engineers, teachers, and business owners—who want to invest back home but don't know where to start. They've heard too many horror stories: relatives mismanaging funds, land bought without proper title or abandoned buildings that never reach completion. Their stories are real. Their fears are valid.

This book was born out of a passion to provide clarity, structure, and a proven system that empowers you to invest in Nigerian real estate safely, confidently, and profitably—no matter where in the world you reside. Over the past two decades, I have helped investors avoid costly mistakes and build solid portfolios in Nigeria, using a practical and professional approach. What you'll find in these pages is not theory—it's a tested formula I've developed and refined over years of helping clients succeed.

The Diaspora Property Formula™ is your blueprint. Whether you're buying your first plot of land, constructing a family home, or diversifying your wealth portfolio, this book will guide you. Together, we'll move from fear to confidence, from confusion to clarity, and from dreams to deeds.

Thank you for trusting me to walk this journey with you.

INTRODUCTION

Nigerians in the diaspora contribute over $20 billion in remittances every year—an economic lifeline that supports families, drives community development, and fuels national growth. This massive financial flow represents the hopes, dreams, and hard work of millions of Nigerians building better lives abroad while maintaining deep connections to home.

Yet when it comes to real estate investment—one of the most reliable paths to generational wealth—many of these accomplished professionals face a painful dilemma: *"I want to invest in Nigerian property, but how can I do it without being scammed, overcharged, or losing everything I've worked for?"*

The concerns are well-founded. Real estate fraud remains a persistent challenge in Nigeria's property market, with diaspora investors particularly vulnerable due to their distance from the transactions and reliance on intermediaries. Stories of fake land titles, abandoned construction projects, and missing funds have created genuine apprehension among potential investors, keeping many on the sidelines despite their desire to invest back home.

However, this cautionary perspective tells only part of the story. The Central Bank of Nigeria reports that diaspora remittances reached $20.93 billion in 2024, representing an 8.9% increase year-on-year, with a substantial portion channeled into real estate investments. Industry analysts consistently note that diaspora Nigerians represent a major driving force in Nigeria's property market, particularly in premium segments and growth corridors.

The reality is that successful diaspora property investment is not only possible—it's happening every day. Those who succeed don't rely on luck; they follow systematic approaches that minimize risk while maximizing opportunity.

The answer to safe, profitable diaspora property investment is yes—but only if you follow the right process.

The Diaspora Property Formula™ (DPF) is a comprehensive, three-pillar strategic approach I developed specifically for diaspora investors after two decades of successful client representation: **Plan with Precision, Pick with Purpose**, and **Protect with Power**. Each pillar contains essential frameworks, tools, checklists, and safeguards that transform property investment from a risky gamble into a systematic wealth-building strategy.

This book will teach you how to:

- Understand why Nigerian property remains one of the world's most compelling investment opportunities despite the challenges
- Identify and avoid the critical traps that destroy diaspora real estate investments
- Build a professional team you can trust and hold accountable from thousands of miles away
- Navigate legal requirements and secure clean property titles without being physically present
- Manage and optimize your property investments from anywhere in the world
- Structure your investments to create lasting wealth and meaningful legacy for future generations

If you've ever felt torn between the desire to invest in Nigeria and legitimate concerns about security and transparency, this book will provide the confidence, clarity, and systematic approach you need to succeed.

Nigerian property investment isn't just about buying land or buildings—it's about maintaining your connection to home, creating generational wealth, and participating in one of Africa's most dynamic growth stories.

Your journey from uncertainty to ownership, from concern to confidence, and from dreams to deeds begins now.

Let's unlock the power of the Diaspora Property Formula™ and build your Nigerian property success story together.

Part I

PLAN WITH PRECISION

This section prepares you to succeed by laying a solid foundation for your investment journey.

You'll uncover the reasons to invest, understand the pitfalls to avoid, prepare financially, and dismantle common myths that have held others back.

CHAPTER ONE

WHY INVEST IN NIGERIA PROPERTY?

For Nigerians living abroad, the pull of home often goes beyond mere nostalgia. It represents opportunity, connection, and legacy. While Nigeria's economy has faced challenges in recent years, the fundamentals for property investment remain compelling. With an estimated population of 216 million and growing, Nigeria continues to offer one of the most dynamic real estate markets on the African continent.

The opportunity to own property in Nigeria is not only sentimental—it is strategic. The Nigerian real estate market, valued at $91.1 million in 2023 and projected to reach $137.8 million by 2030 with a compound annual growth rate of 6.1%, offers substantial returns particularly in growth cities like Lagos, Abuja, Port Harcourt, and emerging hubs like Ibadan and Uyo. Yet many Nigerians abroad remain on the sidelines, unsure of how to navigate the system, who to trust, and where to start.

Three Big Reasons to Invest Now

1. Explosive Population Growth

Nigeria's demographic trajectory is nothing short of remarkable. The United Nations Population Fund confirms that Nigeria's population is expected to reach 400 million by 2050, making it the third most populous country in the world. This represents a 54% increase from current levels—more people inevitably mean more housing demand. The current annual growth rate of 3.2% is driven by a total fertility rate of 5.3, creating sustained pressure on housing infrastructure that smart investors can capitalize on.

This population boom isn't just about numbers—it's about a growing middle class with increasing purchasing power. As Nigeria's economy stabilizes and grows, projected at 6.91% annually through 2029 according to market forecasts, this demographic dividend translates directly into housing demand across all segments of the market.

2. Rapid Urban Expansion

Nigeria's urbanization story is accelerating rapidly. In 2024, 53% of Nigerians lived in urban areas, up from previous years, creating unprecedented demand for city housing that consistently outpaces supply. This urban migration trend shows no signs of slowing, with young Nigerians continuing to move from rural areas to cities in search of better economic opportunities.

Property values in suburbs and satellite towns are rising as city centers become increasingly unaffordable for middle-income earners. This creates a ripple effect of opportunity for investors who position themselves in emerging corridors and growth areas ahead of the curve. University cities, industrial hubs, and areas with good transportation links are seeing particularly strong growth, with some sectors recording increases of over 11% in rental yields. As major cities like Lagos, Abuja and Port Harcourt become more unaffordable this forces people to move to nearby areas and cities.

3. Diaspora Financial Leverage

As a Nigerian in the diaspora, you possess unique advantages that many local investors lack. Your foreign income provides you with stronger purchasing power, especially given recent naira devaluations. This currency advantage allows you to negotiate better deals and access higher-quality properties that might be beyond the reach of local buyers operating solely in naira.

Additionally, your access to foreign credit markets, international banking relationships, and often more stable income streams means you can invest more strategically. You can weather market fluctuations better and take advantage of opportunities when others might be forced to sell. This financial leverage, combined with your emotional connection to the country, positions you perfectly to build a substantial property portfolio.

Beyond Investment: Emotional and Legacy Value

For many diaspora Nigerians, real estate investment transcends mere financial returns. It represents a tangible connection to home—a way to maintain roots while building bridges for future generations. Whether it's securing land for a retirement home where you can return in your golden years, or establishing rental properties that provide passive income while you're abroad, or building a home for your parent , property ownership offers both emotional satisfaction and financial security.

The psychological benefits are significant too. Owning property in Nigeria provides a sense of belonging and achievement that resonates deeply with the diaspora experience. It's about establishing a presence in your homeland and leaving something meaningful behind for your children—a foundation they can build upon, whether they choose to return to Nigeria or simply maintain the family's connection to its roots.

The Time is Now

Nigeria's real estate market stands at an inflection point. Current economic challenges have created opportunities for savvy investors who can see beyond short-term volatility to long-term potential. The fundamentals—population growth, urbanization, and infrastructure development—remain incredibly strong.

With property prices in many markets still recovering from recent economic adjustments, and with your unique position as a diaspora investor, the timing has rarely been better to establish your foothold in Nigeria's property market. The question isn't whether to invest, but rather how to do it smartly, safely, and strategically.

The pages that follow will show you exactly how to navigate this opportunity, avoid the common pitfalls that trap unwary investors, and build a property portfolio that serves both your financial goals and your deeper connection to Nigeria. Your journey as a diaspora property investor in Nigeria starts here.

THE PROPERTY TRAPS YOU MUST AVOID

One of the realities of investing in Nigeria is that most of the landmines are predictable, avoidable traps. It is possible to avoid these traps if you learn from the experience of others and follow a proven process for real estate investment. The good news? Every trap has a solution, and awareness is your first line of defense.

The Five Most Dangerous Property Traps

1. The Family Member Trap

Most diaspora investors approach property investment from a personal point of view rather than seeing it as a business process. "My cousin will handle everything. I trust family more than strangers." This sentiment, while understandable, has cost diaspora Nigerians millions of dollars. The Family Member Trap occurs when you assign a relative to buy, supervise, or manage a property transaction without clear accountability, documentation, or professional oversight.

The problem isn't that family members are inherently dishonest—most aren't. The issue is that emotional trust becomes a substitute for legal clarity and professional competence. Your well-meaning uncle might genuinely intend to help, but without proper contracts, clear payment schedules, and documented responsibilities, even the most honest relative can make costly mistakes or face situations they're not equipped to handle. Most family members also realize that there will be no consequence for shoddy work, fraud, or carelessness. When you engage professionals or neutral third parties, you can demand greater levels of accountability.

Protection strategy: If you must involve family members, professionalize the relationship. Create written agreements or document your instructions, establish clear roles and responsibilities, require regular reporting, and always use independent verification of all claims and progress. If they are not comfortable with this arrangement or you will feel uncomfortable holding them accountable, you should reconsider working with such a family member, friend, or relative.

2. The Fake Land Title Trap

Nigeria's complex land ownership system, governed by the Land Use Act of 1978, creates opportunities for fraudsters to exploit uninformed buyers. Some fraudulent property companies share fake coordinates of their estate just to deceive buyers, and fake land papers lead to fake search results. The truth is that most diaspora investors are unaware of the various title types or how to verify them.

Key vulnerability points include:

- Land under government acquisition that owners are unaware of
- Properties with disputed ownership or family inheritance conflicts
- Forged or duplicated title documents
- Land in areas without proper government allocation or excision

Protection strategy: A land with a Certificate of Occupancy (C of O) in Lagos, for example, can be verified by taking the C of O number to the Land Bureau at Alausa to confirm if the C of O is in their database. Verifying a land title at the Land Registry typically takes a few days, but this small investment in time and money can save you from catastrophic losses. Always insist on independent verification through qualified legal professionals.

3. The Too-Good-To-Be-True Offer

When desperation meets opportunity, rational thinking often disappears. The Too-Good-To-Be-True Trap preys on your fear of missing out and your desire to maximize returns with your foreign currency advantage. If prime Lagos land is selling for what seems like 30% below market value, or a developer is offering "special diaspora prices" that seem impossibly attractive, alarm bells should ring. There are some questionable promotions like "Buy-one-get-one-free" offers that should be properly investigated.

These offers often come with artificial urgency: "This price is only available this week," or "We have other diaspora clients interested." The pressure to act quickly prevents proper due diligence and creates conditions for poor decision-making.

Common variations include:

- "Distress sales" that aren't actually distressed
- "Government allocations" being sold below market rate
- "Insider deals" from developers with questionable track records
- Properties priced in foreign currency but with hidden conversion manipulations

Protection strategy: If the deal seems too good to be true, it probably is. Always compare prices across multiple legitimate sources, take time for thorough investigation regardless of artificial deadlines, and remember that legitimate good deals are rare but not impossible—they just require extra verification.

4. The Developer Delay Trap

Off-plan property purchases can offer excellent value, but they also expose you to the Developer Delay Trap—paying for properties that are never completed or are delivered years behind schedule with no recourse. The approval process for projects in Nigeria has many bureaucratic bottlenecks and is very costly. Many developers touting off-plan products do not have the resources to meet these requirements and often sell the hype without any proper approvals. When you're paying from abroad, it's easy for developers to string you along with photos of "progress" and promises of completion dates that keep shifting.

Red flags include:

- Developers without verifiable track records of completed projects
- Payment schedules that front-load too much money before construction milestones
- Contracts without clear penalty clauses for delays
- Projects without proper government approvals and building permits

Protection strategy: Research the developer's history thoroughly, insist on milestone-based payments with funds held in escrow, include penalty clauses for delays in all contracts, and use local professionals to provide independent progress reports.

5. The Verbal Agreement Trap

"Don't worry, we'll handle the paperwork later. Let's just start with a handshake." In Nigeria's relationship-based business culture, verbal agreements and informal understandings are common. However, for diaspora investors, the Verbal Agreement Trap can be financially devastating.

Without written contracts, you have no legal recourse when things go wrong. Memories fade, circumstances change, and what seemed like a clear understanding can become a source of costly disputes. The challenge is compounded when you're dealing across time zones and can't be physically present for regular face-to-face meetings.

Common situations include:

- Payment schedules agreed to verbally but not documented
- Property specifications and finishing standards left undefined

- Maintenance and management responsibilities not clearly outlined
- Profit-sharing arrangements in joint ventures without written terms

Protection strategy: Nothing should be left to spoken promises. Every agreement, no matter how small, should be documented in writing and signed by all parties. Use email to confirm verbal discussions, create detailed contracts for all transactions, and maintain comprehensive records of all communications.

CTA – Reflect & Act:

Personal Reflection Questions:

- Have I ever heard of or experienced one of these traps? What lesson did I learn?
- Which trap am I most susceptible to based on my personality and circumstances?
- What due diligence steps will I never skip again?
- Who do I currently trust with property advice, and do they have the professional qualifications to deserve that trust?

Action Steps:

1. Identify and research qualified professionals in your target investment area
2. Create a personal due diligence checklist based on the guidelines in this chapter
3. Set up systems for ongoing monitoring of any current investments
4. Review any existing property investments for vulnerability to these traps

Next Steps:

- Visit www.diasporapropertyformula.com/workbook to complete your "Risk Assessment" worksheet

CHAPTER THREE

PICKING THE RIGHT LOCATION AND PROPERTY

Location is everything in real estate, and this truth is amplified when you're investing from thousands of miles away. Nigerian property prices are experiencing significant upward momentum across major cities, with Lagos leading at 39.5% growth in 2024, but the right property in the wrong location can still become a financial drain, while a modest property in a great location can become a goldmine. For diasporans, the location question is even more critical—you're not on ground to see changes or shifts in community development in real time.

The Science of Location Selection

The most successful diaspora property investors don't just buy in cities they know—they buy in growth corridors within those cities. Land values in high-growth corridors like Epe, Ibeju-Lekki, and Mowe have appreciated by over 200% in the past five years, with investors who purchase land early in developing areas often seeing returns exceeding 400% within a decade.

Understanding urban expansion patterns is crucial. Lagos, with its booming population and economic activities, continues to expand its commercial and residential spaces, while Abuja remains a political and luxury real estate hub. These cities aren't growing randomly—they're expanding along predictable corridors driven by infrastructure development and government planning.

Key Factors to Consider When Choosing a Location

1. Proximity to Growth Infrastructure

Infrastructure development is the strongest predictor of property appreciation. Look for areas near new roads, bridges, rail lines, airports, or major industrial projects. The Lagos-Ibadan Expressway, Lekki Deep Sea Port, and the ongoing Lagos-Calabar Coastal Highway projects are creating massive opportunities for early investors.

As Lagos continues to expand, areas like Mowe, Ofada, and Shimawa are gaining attention due to their proximity to major transportation corridors. When government announces major infrastructure projects, smart investors position themselves along these corridors before prices reflect the coming development.

Key infrastructure indicators to watch:

- New road projects and expressway extensions
- Airport development and expansion plans
- Industrial zone designations
- Educational institution developments
- Healthcare facility expansions

2. Urban Expansion Corridors

Cities like Lagos, Abuja, and Port Harcourt are expanding along predictable paths. Understanding these expansion patterns gives you a significant advantage in location selection.

Lagos Expansion Patterns:

- **Eastward Growth**: The Lekki axis has been described as "the fastest-growing corridor in the West African sub-region"
- **Northward Movement**: Areas like Mowe, Ofada, and along the Lagos-Ibadan corridor
- **Island Development**: Continued premium development on Victoria Island and Ikoyi

Abuja Expansion Trends: Satellite towns like Gwarimpa, Jahi, Katampe, and newer districts are experiencing rapid development as the city center becomes increasingly expensive.

Port Harcourt Growth Areas: Rumuodumaya, Eliozu, and other satellite communities are emerging as middle-class residential hubs.

3. Security and Accessibility Assessment

Physical security and consistent access are non-negotiable factors, especially for diaspora investors who can't monitor their investments daily. Research crime statistics, flooding history, and seasonal accessibility challenges.

Critical security factors:

- Proximity to police stations and security posts
- Gated community development trends in the area
- Street lighting and general infrastructure
- Community association strength and organization

Accessibility considerations:

- Multiple route options to avoid single-point-of-failure access
- Public transportation availability
- Road quality during rainy seasons
- Distance from major commercial centers

4. Title and Documentation Clarity

The real estate sector experienced a 5.4% growth rate in Q3 2024, with industry analysts predicting 6-8% growth in 2025, but this growth is concentrated in areas with clear, uncontested titles. The more developed and regularized the location, the higher the chance of clean titles and smooth transactions.

Established areas with existing infrastructure typically have clearer title documentation, while frontier areas may offer better prices but come with higher documentation risks. Balance opportunity with security based on your risk tolerance and investment timeline.

How to Pick the Right Property Type

Your property selection should align with your specific investment strategy and personal circumstances.

Investment Strategy Alignment:

Buy and Hold for Appreciation:

- Focus on land in growth corridors
- Target areas with 5-10 year development timelines
- Prioritize locations over current structures
- Consider agricultural land with urban expansion potential

Rent and Earn Strategy:

- Choose completed or near-completed residential properties
- Target middle-class residential areas with consistent demand
- Prioritize properties with modern amenities
- Consider proximity to business districts and educational institutions

Build to Live Eventually:

- Select residential land in established or rapidly developing areas
- Ensure compliance with building regulations and zoning
- Consider climate, community, and lifestyle factors
- Plan for gradual development to spread costs over time

Budget and Payment Flexibility Considerations:

Land vs. Built Property Decision Matrix:

Choose Land When:

- You have a longer investment timeline (5+ years)
- You want maximum appreciation potential
- You have the patience for development planning
- Your budget allows for gradual improvement over time

Choose Built Property When:

- You need immediate rental income
- You prefer lower management complexity
- You want to live in or rent the property within 2-3 years
- You have limited time for development oversight

The 5-Point Location Scorecard System

Successful diaspora investors use systematic approaches to evaluate potential locations. Here's a proven framework for comparing investment opportunities:

Scorecard Categories (Rate 1-5 for each):

1. Infrastructure Development Score:

- Current road quality and access
- Planned infrastructure projects
- Utilities availability (electricity, water, internet)
- Transportation links to major centers

2. Growth Trajectory Score:

- Population growth trends in the area
- New business development
- Government investment and support

- Educational and healthcare facility development

3. Security and Stability Score:

- Crime statistics and trends
- Community organization strength
- Environmental risks (flooding, erosion)
- Political stability and government support

4. Title and Legal Clarity Score:

- Documentation completeness
- History of land disputes in the area
- Government recognition and support
- Ease of obtaining necessary approvals

5. Investment Fundamentals Score:

- Current price relative to comparable areas
- Rental yield potential
- Resale market activity
- Currency and economic stability factors

Scoring Guidelines:

- **20-25 points**: Excellent investment opportunity
- **15-19 points**: Good opportunity with manageable risks
- **10-14 points**: Proceed with caution and additional research
- **Below 10 points**: Consider alternative locations

Regional Investment Opportunities

Lagos Investment Zones:

Premium Growth Areas:

- Ibeju-Lekki: Industrial and residential development hub
- Victoria Island Extension: Continued luxury development

- Yaba: Technology and innovation district

Emerging Value Areas:

- Mowe-Ofada Corridor: Transportation and industrial growth
- Epe: Tourism and residential development
- Ajah: Middle-class residential expansion

Abuja Investment Opportunities:

Established Premium Areas:

- Asokoro, Maitama, Wuse 2: Government and diplomatic housing
- Gwarimpa: Middle to upper-middle-class residential

Growth Areas:

- Jahi, Katampe: Emerging middle-class districts
- Kuje, Gwagwalada: Affordable housing expansion
- Airport Road Corridor: Commercial development

Secondary City Opportunities:

Port Harcourt:

- GRA areas for premium investments
- Ada George and Eliozu for middle-class residential

Kano:

- Industrial areas around manufacturing zones
- Residential expansion in planned districts

Making the Final Decision

After evaluating locations using the scorecard system, consider these final decision factors:

Personal Factors:

- Your emotional connection to specific areas
- Family and social network considerations
- Long-term retirement or relocation plans
- Risk tolerance and investment timeline

Market Timing:

- Current price cycles in your target areas
- Infrastructure project timelines
- Economic and political stability factors
- Currency exchange considerations

Professional Support:

- Availability of qualified professionals in the area
- Local market knowledge and support networks
- Property management service quality
- Legal and regulatory compliance support

CHAPTER FOUR

LEGAL LANDMINES AND HOW TO AVOID THEM

B uying property in Nigeria without proper legal due diligence is like jumping out of a plane without a parachute. The legal landscape is complex, the stakes are high, and the consequences of mistakes can be financially devastating. Land fraud, double allocation, encroachment, and litigation risks are real threats, but they can all be avoided with proper knowledge and professional support.

The Nigerian legal system governing real estate is built on the Land Use Act of 1978, which vests all land in state governments. This creates a unique legal environment where understanding the proper procedures isn't just helpful—it's essential for protecting your investment.

Essential Legal Terms Every Diaspora Investor Must Understand

Before diving into the landmines, you must understand the fundamental legal documents and concepts that govern Nigerian real estate transactions.

1. Deed of Assignment

This is your proof of legal transfer of ownership from the seller to you. It must be properly executed, stamped, and registered to be legally valid. The Deed of Assignment should clearly identify the parties, describe the property accurately, state the consideration (purchase price), and be signed by both parties in the presence of witnesses.

Critical elements that must be present:

- Full legal description of the property including survey coordinates
- Clear chain of title from the original allocation
- Proper execution with signatures and witnesses
- Evidence of stamp duty payment
- Registration at the appropriate land registry

2. Survey Plan

This document shows the exact location, dimensions, and boundaries of the land. It should be prepared by a registered surveyor and must correlate exactly with the coordinates mentioned in other title documents.

Key verification points:

- Survey must be current
- Surveyor must be licensed and in good standing
- Coordinates must match exactly with other documents
- Physical beacons should be visible and correspond to the survey

3. Certificate of Occupancy (C of O)

Issued by the state government, this document confirms the legal right to occupy and use the land for a specified period and purpose. The C of O is the strongest form of title in Nigeria and should be the ultimate goal of any serious property investor.

Understanding C of O variations:

- **Statutory C of O**: Issued for original allocations, strongest form of title
- **Customary C of O**: For customary land converted to statutory title
- **Deemed C of O**: For land with perfected title but certificate not yet issued

4. Governor's Consent

Required when land with a C of O is transferred after the first assignment. This consent legitimizes the transfer and updates government records. Obtaining Governor's Consent can take 6-18 months and involves significant fees, but it's essential for clean title transfer.

Governor's Consent process:

- Application with required documents
- Property valuation by government officials
- Payment of consent fees (typically 3-5% of property value)
- Issuance of consent letter and updated documentation

Legal Landmines That Destroy Diaspora Investments

Landmine #1: Government Acquisition Trap

One of the most devastating traps involves buying land that's under government acquisition or earmarked for public use. Even if you have seemingly legitimate documents, the government can revoke land under acquisition, often with minimal compensation.

How to protect yourself:

- Check the state government's official gazette for acquisition notices
- Verify that your target area isn't designated for public projects
- Engage local government officials for informal confirmation
- Use legal professionals familiar with local government plans

Landmine #2: Skipping Professional Title Search

Many diaspora investors rely on documents provided by sellers without conducting independent verification. Title searches at the Land Registry are essential for confirming legitimate ownership and identifying potential problems.

Comprehensive title search includes:

- Verification of seller's ownership through chain of title
- Check for existing mortgages, liens, or encumbrances
- Confirmation that all taxes and fees are current
- Verification of compliance with zoning regulations

Landmine #3: Unqualified Legal Representation

Using inexperienced or unqualified people can be more dangerous than using no lawyer at all. Real estate law in Nigeria is specialized, and freelancers may miss critical issues.

Selecting qualified legal representation:

- Choose lawyers specializing in real estate with verifiable track records
- Request references from recent diaspora clients
- Ensure they have relationships with relevant government agencies

Landmine #4: Informal Payment and Documentation

Making any payments without proper receipts, contracts, or documentation creates vulnerability to fraud and makes legal recourse difficult or impossible.

Proper documentation requirements:

- Written purchase agreements signed by all parties
- Official receipts for all payments made
- Bank transfer records for payment verification
- Photographic evidence of property condition and boundaries

The Legal Protection Framework

Phase 1: Pre-Purchase Legal Due Diligence

Before making any financial commitments, conduct comprehensive legal verification:

Document Authentication:

- Verify all documents with issuing authorities
- Confirm authenticity of signatures and official stamps
- Cross-check information across multiple documents
- Validate surveyor and lawyer credentials

Ownership Verification:

- Trace title history back to original government allocation
- Confirm seller's legal right to transfer the property
- Verify that all previous transfers were properly executed
- Check for any disputes or litigation history

Regulatory Compliance Check:

- Confirm compliance with local zoning laws
- Verify building approvals if applicable
- Check environmental compliance requirements
- Ensure all taxes and fees are current

Phase 2: Transaction Structure and Execution

Contract Development:

- Create comprehensive purchase agreements
- Include specific performance milestones and deadlines
- Establish clear penalty clauses for non-performance
- Define dispute resolution mechanisms

Payment Structure:

- Structure payments to minimize exposure
- Require documentation before each payment release
- Maintain detailed records of all transactions

Closing Process:

- Coordinate simultaneous document execution and payment
- Ensure immediate registration of transfer documents
- Obtain all original documents before final payment
- Conduct final property inspection before closing

Phase 3: Post-Purchase Protection

Immediate Actions:

- Register all documents with appropriate authorities
- Begin Governor's Consent application process if required
- Update property records with your information
- Establish security arrangements for the property

Ongoing Protection:

- Maintain regular communication with local authorities
- Monitor for any government acquisition notices
- Keep all documentation in secure, accessible locations
- Establish relationships with local legal and real estate professionals

Red Flags That Signal Legal Problems

Document Red Flags:

- Photocopied documents without originals
- Inconsistent information across different documents
- Missing signatures, stamps, or official seals
- Recent date changes or obvious alterations

Seller Behavior Red Flags:

- Pressure to complete transactions quickly
- Reluctance to provide complete documentation
- Unwillingness to meet at official locations

Property Red Flags:

- Lack of clear boundary markers or disputes with neighbors
- Evidence of ongoing construction without apparent permits
- Multiple sellers claiming ownership of the same property
- Unusual pricing that seems too good to be true

Tip

Choose a qualified property lawyer with specific expertise in diaspora transactions and a track record of successful completions.

Local Representatives: Establish relationships with trustworthy local professionals who can act as your eyes and ears on the ground.

When you get the legal part right, you build on solid ground—literally and figuratively. The investment in proper legal protection is minimal compared to the potential losses from cutting corners on due diligence and professional support.

CTA – Reflect & Act:

Legal Preparedness Questions:

- Have I verified title documents before? What was missing from my process?
- Who is my current go-to real estate lawyer in Nigeria, and are they truly qualified?
- What legal mistakes have I seen others make that I want to avoid?
- Do I have systems in place for ongoing legal monitoring of my investments?

Action Steps:

1. Research and identify qualified real estate lawyers in your target investment areas
2. Create a legal due diligence checklist based on the guidelines in this chapter
3. Establish relationships with real estate lawyer and engage them for document verification
4. Set up systems for ongoing legal compliance monitoring

Use the Legal Checklist in the DPF Workbook to prepare systematically for your next property deal and ensure you never skip critical legal protections.

Part II

PICK WITH PURPOSE

This section walks you through the critical steps of selecting, evaluating, and acquiring the right property in the right place, with the right people.

These chapters turn theory into execution by helping you navigate market opportunities, negotiation, and professional team building.

CHAPTER FIVE

HOW TO USE PAYMENT PLANS AND FINANCING TOOLS

O ne of the biggest myths among diaspora Nigerians is that you need a massive lump sum to invest in Nigerian real estate. While having cash certainly provides negotiating leverage, structured payment plans and creative financing options can make property investment accessible even on a modest income. The key is understanding which financing tools align with your investment strategy and risk tolerance.

The Nigerian financing landscape presents both opportunities and challenges for diaspora investors. Unlike developed markets with robust mortgage systems, Nigeria's mortgage terms are typically 10-15 years with double-digit interest rates. Government mortgage options remain limited, and the application processes are often cumbersome and time-consuming. This financing gap has led banks, developers, and sellers to adopt creative payment structures and installment plans, though these options often increase transaction costs and may carry additional risks.

Understanding Your Financing Options

1. Developer Payment Plans

Many reputable developers now offer structured payment plans ranging from 6 to 24 months, often with minimal interest charges. These plans make premium properties accessible while spreading financial commitment over manageable periods.

Typical payment structure:

- Initial deposit: 20-30% to secure the property
- Construction milestone payments: 40-50% as work progresses
- Completion payment: 20-30% upon handover

Key advantages:

- Access to pre-appreciation pricing on new developments
- Ability to inspect progress before final payment
- Developer warranties on construction quality
- Often includes property management services

Critical considerations:

- Research the developer's track record thoroughly
- Understand all fees and penalties for late payments
- Verify construction permits and government approvals
- Confirm when ownership actually transfers to you

2. Government-Backed Programs

The Nigerian government has developed specific programs to facilitate diaspora property investment, though availability and terms change frequently.

National Housing Fund (NHF) and Federal Mortgage Bank Programs: These programs offer diaspora-specific financing options with potentially favorable terms compared to commercial alternatives. However, program details, eligibility requirements, and loan limits are subject to change.

Potential benefits:

- Lower interest rates than commercial options
- Government backing provides additional security
- Formal documentation and legal protection
- Structured repayment schedules

Important note: For current program details, terms, and eligibility requirements, contact the Federal Mortgage Bank of Nigeria (FMBN) or the Nigerians in Diaspora Commission (NiDCOM) directly, as these programs evolve frequently.

3. Commercial Bank Financing

Nigerian banks offer mortgage facilities, though with higher interest rates and shorter terms than international markets. Interest rates are typically double-digit with loan terms of 10-15 years.

What banks look for:

- Stable income and employment with reputable organizations
- Good credit history and financial standing
- Adequate collateral or guarantees
- Clear repayment capacity

Benefits of bank financing:

- Faster approval processes than government programs
- Established legal frameworks and documentation
- Professional loan management and servicing

Key considerations:

- Review all terms carefully for hidden charges
- Understand prepayment penalties and default consequences

- Compare offers from multiple banks
- Ensure you can handle double-digit interest rates

4. Cooperative and Group Investment

Pooling resources with other diaspora investors can provide access to larger properties while spreading risk across multiple participants.

Cooperative societies offer particular advantages for aspiring investors. Most cooperatives charge single-digit interest rates and approve loans to members faster than banks or financial institutions. If you're planning real estate investment, joining a reliable cooperative society is highly recommended.

Group investment strategies:

- Partner with family members or trusted associates
- Join structured diaspora investment clubs
- Pool resources for premium properties individually unaffordable
- Share risks and management responsibilities

Success factors:

- Clear legal agreements defining ownership shares
- Professional management of the investment vehicle
- Transparent accounting and reporting systems
- Defined exit strategies for individual participants

Risk Management and Financial Planning

Smart Money Management Principles

Diversification rules:

- Never commit more than 30% of available capital to a single property
- Spread financing across different arrangements
- Maintain emergency reserves for unexpected costs

Currency considerations:

- Understand how exchange rate fluctuations affect payment obligations
- Build currency buffers into payment planning
- Consider the natural hedge your foreign income provides

Documentation essentials:

- Maintain comprehensive records of all payments and agreements
- Ensure all financing arrangements are properly documented
- Keep original documents in secure, accessible locations

Common Financing Pitfalls to Avoid

Hidden costs and fees: Always request complete fee schedules including administrative fees, late payment penalties, documentation costs, and currency conversion charges.

Unclear ownership transfer: Understand exactly when ownership transfers to you. Some plans require full payment before transfer, while others provide proportional ownership as payments are made.

Inadequate refund policies: Ensure clear refund provisions if circumstances change or developers fail to deliver as promised.

Maximizing Your Diaspora Advantage

Your Unique Position

Currency strength: Your foreign income provides natural protection against local currency devaluation, making you an attractive borrower for Nigerian lenders.

Credit profile: International credit history and stable income can provide access to better financing terms than available to local borrowers.

Professional networks: Use your international connections to identify investment opportunities and financing sources not available through traditional channels.

Building Long-term Financial Relationships

Banking strategy: Establish relationships with Nigerian banks that have international operations, making cross-border financing and payments easier to manage.

Professional team: Build relationships with mortgage brokers, financial advisors, and legal professionals who specialize in diaspora property investment.

Developer partnerships: Work with reputable developers who have established financing programs and proven track records of successful project completion.

Creating Your Financing Strategy

Assessment Phase

- Calculate realistic monthly investment capacity
- Determine risk tolerance and investment timeline
- Identify preferred property types and locations
- Research available financing options in target areas

Planning and Execution

- Match financing options to specific goals and circumstances
- Create contingency plans for income changes or unexpected costs
- Start with smaller investments to test systems and relationships
- Build equity and credit history for future opportunities

The most successful diaspora investors understand that financing is not just about getting money—it's about structuring deals that maximize returns while managing risks appropriately. Whether you choose developer payment plans, government programs, bank financing, or cooperative arrangements, the key is matching the right tool to your specific circumstances and investment objectives.

Remember: experienced real estate investors employ different strategies to fund their projects. The goal is not necessarily to avoid debt, but to use leverage wisely to maximize your investment potential while protecting your financial security.

CTA – Reflect & Act:

Financial Planning Questions:

- What is my realistic monthly or quarterly property investment budget?
- Which financing option best matches my investment timeline and risk tolerance?
- Do I have adequate emergency reserves for unexpected costs or payment delays?
- Could I benefit from partnering with others to increase my investment power?

Action Steps:

1. Calculate your true investment capacity including all associated costs
2. Research specific financing programs available for your target property types
3. Establish banking relationships that facilitate international property investment
4. Create contingency plans for currency fluctuations and income changes

Next Steps: Review the Financing Strategy Planner in the DPF Workbook to create a personalized financing approach that maximizes your investment potential while managing risk appropriately. Your financing strategy can be the difference between gradual wealth building and accelerated investment growth.

CHAPTER SIX

THE DIASPORA PROPERTY FORMULA

After working with hundreds of Nigerian investors abroad over the years, observing their successes and learning from their costly mistakes, I developed the Diaspora Property Formula™ (DPF) to simplify and systematically de-risk the process of property investment in Nigeria. This isn't theoretical—it's a battle-tested framework that has helped diaspora investors navigate the complex Nigerian real estate market successfully.

The reality is that most diaspora property investments fail not because of market conditions, but because of poor planning, inadequate research, and lack of systematic approach. The DPF addresses these fundamental issues by providing a structured methodology that works regardless of your budget, location, or experience level.

Why You Need a Systematic Approach

The Nigerian real estate market is experiencing unprecedented growth, with the market projected to grow by 6.91% annually through 2029, resulting in a market volume of US$3.41 trillion by 2029. However, this growth comes with complexity. Over 60% of new residential developments are concentrated in Lagos, Abuja, and Port Harcourt, but not all areas within these cities offer equal opportunity.

Without a systematic approach, diaspora investors often fall into emotional decision-making, investing in areas they remember from childhood rather than current growth corridors, or trusting family recommendations without proper due diligence. The DPF eliminates these risks by providing objective criteria for every investment decision.

The DPF Framework: Three Strategic Pillars

Pillar 1: Plan with Precision

Precision planning is the foundation of successful diaspora property investment. This pillar ensures you invest strategically rather than emotionally, with clear objectives and realistic expectations.

Clarify Your Investment Goals

Before evaluating any property, you must understand exactly what you want to achieve. Different goals require different strategies, timelines, and risk tolerances.

Primary Investment Objectives:

- **Wealth Preservation**: Protecting your foreign-earned income from currency devaluation
- **Income Generation**: Creating rental income streams from abroad
- **Capital Appreciation**: Long-term wealth building through property value increases
- **Legacy Building**: Establishing assets for future generations
- **Retirement Planning**: Preparing for eventual relocation to Nigeria

Time Horizon Considerations:

- **Short-term (1-3 years)**: Focus on liquid properties in established markets
- **Medium-term (3-7 years)**: Target growth corridors with development pipeline
- **Long-term (7+ years)**: Consider frontier areas with transformation potential

Understand Your Financial Capacity

Many diaspora investors overextend themselves by focusing only on property prices without considering total investment requirements. The DPF approach includes comprehensive financial planning.

Total Investment Calculation:

- Property acquisition cost
- Legal and documentation fees (typically 5-10% of property value)
- Development or renovation costs if applicable
- Property management and maintenance reserves
- Currency hedging and transfer costs
- Emergency reserves for unexpected expenses

Cash Flow Analysis:

- Monthly investment capacity based on disposable income
- Impact of exchange rate fluctuations on payment ability
- Rental income projections and collection reliability
- Holding costs during vacancy periods

Research Market Dynamics

Understanding market dynamics in your target area is crucial for timing and pricing decisions. The DPF requires systematic market research before investment.

Economic Indicators to Monitor:

- Population growth and urbanization trends
- Infrastructure development timelines
- Government policy changes affecting property ownership
- Local economic drivers and employment patterns

Market Performance Metrics:

- Historical property price appreciation rates
- Rental yield patterns and vacancy rates
- Construction costs and material availability
- Financing options and interest rate trends

Pillar 2: Pick with Purpose

Purpose-driven property selection ensures you choose investments that align with your goals and risk tolerance while maximizing return potential.

Choose Location Based on Growth, Access, and Future Value

Location selection is the most critical decision in real estate investment. The DPF provides a systematic approach to identify high-potential areas before they become obvious to the broader market.

Growth Indicators Analysis:

- Infrastructure development announcements and timelines
- Corporate relocations and business district expansion
- Educational institution and healthcare facility development
- Government policy support and urban planning initiatives

Accessibility Assessment:

- Multiple transportation route options
- Proximity to business centers and amenities
- Road quality and seasonal accessibility challenges
- Public transportation availability and expansion plans

Future Value Projections:

- Planned developments within 5-kilometer radius
- Zoning changes and land use evolution
- Population density trends and demographic shifts
- Economic activity diversification potential

Select Properties with Secure Documentation and Flexible Payment

The DPF emphasizes documentation quality and payment flexibility as key selection criteria, especially for diaspora investors who cannot monitor transactions daily.

Documentation Security Checklist:

- Clean chain of title from original government allocation
- Current survey plans with registered surveyor certification
- Compliance with local zoning and building regulations
- Absence of litigation, liens, or encumbrances
- Government approvals for intended use

Payment Flexibility Evaluation:

- Structured payment schedules aligned with your cash flow
- Milestone-based payments tied to verifiable progress
- Reasonable penalty structures for delays or changes
- Currency options and exchange rate protection
- Escrow or third-party payment security arrangements

Partner with Professionals You Trust

The DPF recognizes that successful diaspora investment requires a qualified professional team. This isn't about finding the cheapest service providers—it's about building relationships with professionals who understand diaspora needs and can deliver results.

Trust Building Process:

- Verification of professional credentials and licensing
- Reference checks with recent diaspora clients
- Clear service agreements and accountability structures
- Regular communication protocols and reporting systems
- Transparent fee structures without hidden costs

Pillar 3: Protect with Power

Protection ensures your investment remains secure and continues to generate returns over time, despite distance and changing circumstances.

Legally Vet Every Transaction

Legal protection is non-negotiable in Nigerian real estate. The DPF requires comprehensive legal vetting for every aspect of your investment.

Pre-Purchase Legal Review:

- Independent title search and verification
- Due diligence report on seller and property
- Contract review and risk assessment
- Compliance verification with all regulations
- Legal opinion on transaction structure

Transaction Security Measures:

- Proper documentation execution and registration
- Insurance coverage for construction and title risks
- Legal recourse mechanisms for non-performance
- Dispute resolution procedures and jurisdiction
- Post-transaction monitoring and compliance

Maintain Control and Visibility from Abroad

Distance shouldn't mean loss of control. The DPF includes systems for maintaining oversight and decision-making authority regardless of your physical location.

Control Mechanisms:

- Regular reporting schedules with key performance indicators
- Digital monitoring tools and progress tracking systems
- Independent verification processes for all major decisions
- Clear decision-making authority and approval processes
- Emergency response protocols for urgent situations

Visibility Systems:

- Monthly financial reports with photographic evidence
- Quarterly property inspections by independent professionals
- Annual strategic reviews and planning sessions
- Real-time communication channels for urgent matters
- Documentation archival and access systems

Establish Structures to Transfer and Preserve Wealth

The DPF includes wealth preservation strategies that protect your investment from currency devaluation, political changes, and family disputes.

Wealth Preservation Strategies:

- Diversification across property types and locations
- Currency hedging and international banking relationships
- Legal structures for asset protection and succession planning
- Tax optimization strategies for rental income and capital gains
- Emergency liquidation plans for unexpected circumstances

Implementing the DPF Framework

Phase 1: Foundation Building

Plan with Precision Implementation:

- Complete comprehensive financial assessment
- Define specific investment objectives and timelines

- Conduct market research on target areas
- Establish preliminary budget and financing structure

Key Deliverables:

- Investment objectives document
- Financial capacity assessment
- Target market analysis report
- Preliminary investment timeline

Phase 2: Selection and Acquisition

Pick with Purpose Implementation:

- Apply location selection criteria to identify opportunities
- Conduct property due diligence and documentation review
- Assemble professional team and verify credentials
- Structure and negotiate purchase agreements

Key Deliverables:

- Location scorecard analysis
- Property due diligence report
- Professional team agreements
- Purchase contract and payment schedule

Phase 3: Management and Optimization

Protect with Power Implementation:

- Complete legal documentation and registration
- Establish monitoring and reporting systems
- Implement wealth preservation strategies
- Conduct regular performance reviews

Key Deliverables:

- Legal completion

- Monthly monitoring reports
- Annual performance analysis
- Strategic plan updates

Common DPF Implementation Challenges

Challenge 1: Information Overwhelm

Many diaspora investors become paralyzed by the amount of information required for proper due diligence. The key is systematic progression through each pillar rather than trying to analyze everything simultaneously.

Solution: Focus on one pillar at a time, completing all requirements before moving to the next phase.

Challenge 2: Professional Team Building

Finding qualified, trustworthy professionals can be challenging from abroad, especially when dealing with referrals and recommendations.

Solution: Use the DPF's systematic verification process and start with smaller engagements to test relationships before making major commitments.

Challenge 3: Long-Distance Project Management

Maintaining control and oversight of investments from thousands of miles away requires systems and discipline that many investors underestimate.

Solution: Invest in robust communication and monitoring systems from the beginning rather than trying to add them after problems arise.

Measuring DPF Success

Financial Metrics:

- Annual return on investment compared to target benchmarks
- Cash flow generation relative to projections
- Capital appreciation rates versus market averages
- Total cost of ownership compared to budget

Risk Management Metrics:

- Time to complete transactions versus projected timelines
- Number of problems encountered and resolution time
- Professional team performance and reliability scores
- Documentation completeness and legal compliance rates

Strategic Alignment Metrics:

- Progress toward long-term investment objectives
- Portfolio diversification and risk distribution
- Wealth preservation effectiveness against currency devaluation
- Legacy building progress and family satisfaction

The DPF Framework provides the structure and discipline needed for successful diaspora property investment. Each chapter in this book maps directly to specific elements of the framework, ensuring you have the tools and knowledge needed to apply it practically regardless of your starting point.

CTA – Reflect & Act:

Framework Assessment Questions:

- Where am I right now in the DPF cycle? Planning, Picking, or Protecting?
- Which pillar represents my greatest current weakness or knowledge gap?
- What specific actions do I need to take to move forward in my current phase?
- How will I measure the success of my DPF implementation?

Action Steps:

1. Complete the DPF Self-Assessment to identify your current position
2. Create a timeline for implementing each pillar systematically
3. Identify resources and support needed for successful implementation
4. Establish metrics and monitoring systems for tracking progress

Next Steps: Go to the DPF Workbook at www.diasporapropertyformula.com/workbook and complete your Self-Assessment Tracker to create a personalized implementation plan based on your specific circumstances and objectives.

CHAPTER SEVEN

WHERE TO INVEST

Knowing where to invest in Nigerian real estate is often the ultimate deal-breaker. The right city, area, or even specific street can determine your appreciation rate, rental income potential, and investment security. While many diaspora investors gravitate toward familiar areas or follow family recommendations, successful property investment requires objective analysis of growth drivers and market fundamentals.

In 2024, over 60% of new residential developments were concentrated in Lagos, Abuja, and Port Harcourt, but within these major cities, specific corridors and neighborhoods show dramatically different investment potential. Land prices in Old Ikoyi, Lagos, more than doubled between 2021 and 2023, while areas like Sangotedo saw similar exponential growth as developers catered to expanding urban populations. Outside of these major centres are hotspots experiencing growth or likely to experience growth in different parts of the Country. For instance, the Lagos-Calabar Coastal Highway and other infrastructural road projects on-going are already opening up several locations. As the saying goes, the key to making money in real estate is location.

The Strategic Approach to Location Selection

Understanding Growth Patterns

Nigerian cities don't expand randomly—they grow along predictable corridors driven by infrastructure development, government planning, and economic activity. Successful diaspora investors position themselves ahead of these growth patterns rather than chasing areas that have already experienced maximum appreciation.

Primary Growth Drivers:

- Government infrastructure investments
- Corporate relocations and business district expansion
- Educational and healthcare facility development
- Transportation network improvements
- Industrial and economic zone development

Secondary Growth Indicators:

- Middle-class migration patterns
- International company presence
- Shopping and entertainment complex development
- Improved security and urban services
- Real estate developer interest and activity

Hotspot Cities for Diaspora Investment

Lagos: The Commercial Powerhouse

Lagos remains Nigeria's commercial capital and most dynamic real estate market, with prices experiencing 39.5% growth in 2024 and continued appreciation of 5-15% expected through 2025. The city's eastward expansion continues to create exceptional opportunities for strategic investors.

High-Growth Eastern Expansion:

Ibeju-Lekki Corridor: The Lekki axis has been described as "the fastest-growing corridor in the West African sub-region." The convergence of the Dangote Refinery, Lekki Deep Sea Port, and the planned new international airport creates unprecedented development momentum. Land values have appreciated over 300% in the last decade, with continued growth expected as infrastructure projects reach completion.

Investment Opportunities:

- Residential land for future development
- Mixed-use commercial properties
- Industrial and logistics facilities
- Hospitality and tourism-related developments

Ajah and Epe Growth Areas: These areas represent the next tier of Lagos expansion, offering more affordable entry points while benefiting from infrastructure spillover from premium Lekki developments.

Key Features:

- Significantly lower land costs than central Lekki
- Improving transportation links
- Growing middle-class residential demand
- Commercial development following residential growth

Emerging Value Areas:

Mowe-Ofada-Shimawa Corridor: As Lagos continues to expand northward, areas along major transportation corridors in neighboring Ogun State are experiencing rapid appreciation. These areas offer land prices 30-50% cheaper than comparable Lagos locations while benefiting from industrial development and improved infrastructure.

Investment Advantages:

- Strategic land banking opportunities
- Industrial and logistics facility demand

- Residential spillover from Lagos
- Government infrastructure investment

Abuja: The Capital Advantage

As Nigeria's capital, Abuja continues to attract investment in luxury housing and mixed-use developments, with moderate price increases of 8-10% annually forecasted. The city's status as the political and administrative center provides stability and consistent demand drivers.

Established Premium Areas:

Central Districts (Asokoro, Maitama, Wuse): These areas remain the premium residential and commercial zones, attracting government officials, diplomatic missions, and corporate headquarters.

Investment Characteristics:

- Stable, appreciating property values
- High-end residential rental demand
- Commercial and office space requirements
- Limited new development opportunities due to scarcity

High-Growth Satellite Areas:

Gwarimpa, Lokogoma, and Lugbe: These satellite towns are attracting middle to upper-middle-class residents seeking more space and affordability while maintaining reasonable access to central Abuja.

Growth Drivers:

- Expanding middle-class population
- Improved transportation links
- Shopping and commercial development
- International school and healthcare facilities

Emerging Districts:

Guzape, Katampe, and Jahi: These newer districts have recorded a 40% increase in property values over the last five years, driven by planned infrastructure development and high-end residential projects.

Investment Potential:

- Early-stage development opportunities
- Premium residential demand
- Commercial and mixed-use development
- Infrastructure-driven appreciation

Port Harcourt: The Energy Hub

Though historically volatile due to security concerns, Port Harcourt offers high rental yields for commercial and serviced apartments, particularly in areas serving the oil and gas industry. The city's role as Nigeria's energy capital provides consistent demand from corporate tenants.

Investment Considerations:

Strengths:

- High rental yields (often 10-15% annually)
- Corporate tenant demand
- Limited quality accommodation supply
- Government stabilization efforts

Challenges:

- Security concerns in certain areas
- Infrastructure limitations
- Economic volatility tied to oil prices
- Limited residential market growth

Strategic Areas:

- GRA and other secure residential zones
- Areas near major oil company offices

- Serviced apartment locations for corporate housing
- Commercial properties in business districts

Secondary Cities: Hidden Gems

Abeokuta, Ibadan, and Asaba represent excellent opportunities for buy-and-hold strategies or retirement planning, offering more affordable entry points with solid long-term potential.

Ibadan - Academic and Commercial Hub: As Nigeria's third-largest city, Ibadan offers:

- University-driven rental demand
- Industrial development opportunities
- Growing middle-class population
- Relatively affordable property prices

Abeokuta - Industrial Spillover: Benefiting from Lagos proximity:

- Industrial development from Lagos overflow
- Agricultural processing opportunities
- Government support for development
- Transportation link improvements

Asaba - River Niger Advantage: Strategic location benefits:

- Cross-river trade opportunities
- Government investment in infrastructure
- Growing commercial activity
- Affordable land and development costs

How to Identify High-Growth Areas

Follow Infrastructure Development

Infrastructure development is the most reliable predictor of property appreciation. Government announcements of major projects often precede property price increases by 2-3 years, providing opportunity for strategic investors.

Key Infrastructure Indicators:

- Road construction and expressway projects
- Airport development and expansion
- Railway and mass transit projects
- Port and logistics facility development
- Power grid and utility improvements

Research Methods:

- Monitor government budget announcements
- Track contract awards for major projects
- Follow international development bank funding
- Subscribe to infrastructure industry publications
- Maintain relationships with government liaison professionals

Research Current Land Prices vs. Projected Value

Understanding the relationship between current prices and projected future values helps identify undervalued opportunities before they become obvious to the broader market.

Price Analysis Framework:

- Compare current prices to similar areas with existing infrastructure
- Analyze appreciation rates in comparable development corridors
- Factor in construction and development costs
- Consider timeline for infrastructure completion and impact

Valuation Methods:

- Comparable sales analysis in similar growth corridors
- Development cost approach for vacant land
- Income approach for rental properties

- Government valuation data for tax assessment purposes

Look at Commercial Activities and Migration Trends

Commercial activity and population migration patterns provide leading indicators of residential property demand and price appreciation potential.

Commercial Activity Indicators:

- New business registrations and corporate relocations
- Shopping center and retail development
- Bank branch and ATM installations
- Telecommunications infrastructure investment
- Healthcare and educational facility development

Migration Pattern Analysis:

- Population growth statistics from census data
- Employment opportunity creation
- Transportation pattern changes
- School enrollment and healthcare usage trends
- Utility connection and service expansion

Verification and Due Diligence

Never rely solely on promotional materials or second-hand information when evaluating potential investment areas.

Independent Verification Methods:

- On-site inspections by qualified professionals
- Satellite imagery analysis for development progress
- Local government office visits for permit and planning verification
- Multiple real estate agent consultations
- Community leader and resident interviews

The DPF Hotspot Radar Tool

The Diaspora Property Formula includes a systematic scoring tool for evaluating investment locations objectively.

Scoring Categories (1-5 scale):

1. Infrastructure Development Score

- Current infrastructure quality
- Announced infrastructure projects
- Government funding commitments
- Project timeline and completion probability

2. Economic Growth Score

- Employment opportunity creation
- Business development and corporate presence
- Economic diversity and stability
- Government economic support

3. Demographics and Migration Score

- Population growth trends
- Age and income demographics
- Migration patterns and reasons
- Educational and professional workforce

4. Market Fundamentals Score

- Current property price levels
- Historical appreciation rates
- Rental demand and yield potential
- Market liquidity and transaction volume

5. Risk Assessment Score

- Security and stability factors
- Environmental and climate risks
- Political and regulatory stability

- Market volatility and downside protection

Interpretation Guide:

- **20-25 points**: Exceptional investment opportunity
- **15-19 points**: Strong investment potential with manageable risks
- **10-14 points**: Average opportunity requiring additional analysis
- **Below 10 points**: High-risk investment requiring special circumstances

Investment Strategy Alignment

Quick Returns Strategy

Focus on established areas with high transaction volumes and proven appreciation patterns.

Areas:

- Established Lagos corridors (Lekki, Victoria Island extensions)
- Abuja satellite towns with completed infrastructure
- Commercial properties in business districts

Rental Income Strategy

Target areas with consistent rental demand from stable tenant populations.

Optimal Locations:

- University towns and educational districts
- Corporate housing markets near business centers
- Serviced apartment locations in major cities

Long-term Holding Strategy

Identify frontier areas with strong development potential and extended appreciation timelines.

Growth Opportunities:

- Infrastructure development corridors in early stages
- Emerging satellite towns with government support
- Industrial development zones with announced projects

CTA – Reflect & Act:

Investment Strategy Questions:

- What's my primary investment priority: quick returns, rental income, or long-term holding?
- Which growth indicators am I best positioned to monitor and capitalize on?
- How much risk am I willing to accept for higher return potential?
- What timeline works best for my investment and life planning goals?

Action Steps:

1. Use the DPF Hotspot Radar Tool to score your top 3 target locations
2. Conduct independent verification of growth drivers in highest-scoring areas
3. Visit or commission professional inspections of shortlisted properties
4. Create investment timeline and decision criteria for final selection

Next Steps: Choose two target locations to analyze using the DPF Hotspot Radar Tool available in the workbook. Complete comprehensive scoring and create action plans for the highest-potential opportunities that align with your investment strategy.

CHAPTER EIGHT

BUILDING YOUR TRUSTED TEAM

You're in the diaspora. Your property is in Nigeria. Your success depends entirely on the team you build around your investment. This isn't just about finding service providers—it's about creating a network of qualified professionals who understand diaspora challenges and can deliver results when you're thousands of miles away.

The harsh reality is that most diaspora property investments fail not because of market conditions, but because of poor professional relationships, inadequate oversight, and misaligned expectations with local teams. Building the right team isn't an expense—it's the foundation of successful long-distance property investment.

Why Team Building is Critical for Diaspora Investors

The Distance Disadvantage

When you're investing across continents, you cannot rely on personal oversight, daily check-ins, or face-to-face problem-solving. Every decision, every dollar spent, and every milestone achieved depends on professionals acting on your behalf with competence and integrity.

Unique Diaspora Challenges:

- Time zone differences limiting real-time communication
- Cultural and business practice differences
- Currency fluctuations affecting payment timing
- Limited ability to verify claims or progress personally
- Legal recourse complications across jurisdictions

The Trust Multiplication Effect

Each member of your professional team multiplies your capabilities and risk management. A qualified surveyor prevents boundary disputes that could cost millions. A competent project manager saves months of delays and cost overruns. An experienced property lawyer prevents legal problems that could destroy your investment entirely.

The 7 Key Professionals You Need

1. Real Estate Agent/Consultant

Your real estate agent is often your first contact with the Nigerian property market and sets the tone for your entire investment experience. They provide access to deals, market insight, and negotiation skills, but agent quality varies dramatically.

Essential Qualifications: In Nigeria, real estate agents are required to be licensed or registered with relevant professional bodies such as the Nigerian Institution of Estate Surveyors and Valuers (NIESV) or the Real Estate Developers Association of Nigeria (REDAN). Always verify credentials to avoid fraudulent transactions.

What to Look For:

- **Experience with Diaspora Clients**: Understanding of international wire transfers, currency exchange, and remote communication needs
- **Market Specialization**: Deep knowledge of your target areas and property types
- **Professional Network**: Established relationships with other essential team members
- **Technology Adoption**: Use of digital tools for remote property viewing, document sharing, and progress tracking

Red Flags:

- Reluctance to provide professional credentials or references
- Pressure for immediate decisions or payments
- Lack of written agreements or fee transparency
- Limited knowledge of legal requirements or documentation processes

Performance Expectations:

- Transparent commission structure (typically 5-10% of property value)
- Regular market updates and property recommendations
- Assistance with due diligence and verification processes
- Coordination with other professional team members

Please note that in Nigeria, because of lax regulatory enforcement there are several individuals who are not professionals who equally operate as real estate agents or consultants but do not have any credential to show for it. You will deal with a lot of these individuals if you are investing in Nigeria. This is not an issue as you manage your interface with them using a professional.

2. Property Lawyer

Your property lawyer is vital for legal verification, documentation, and protecting your interests. This is not an area to economize—the cost of legal problems far exceeds legal fees.

Specialized Requirements: Choose lawyers specializing in real estate with verifiable track records, preferably with experience serving diaspora clients who understand international banking, currency issues, and remote documentation requirements.

Critical Services:

- **Title Search and Verification**: Independent confirmation of property ownership and legal status
- **Due Diligence Reports**: Comprehensive analysis of legal risks and compliance issues
- **Contract Review and Negotiation**: Protection of your interests in purchase agreements
- **Documentation Management**: Proper execution and registration of all legal documents
- **Dispute Resolution**: Legal recourse for problems or contract breaches
- **Lease agreement preparation and execution**

Quality Indicators:

- Membership in Nigerian Bar Association with good standing
- Specialization in real estate law
- Clear fee structures

3. Licensed Surveyor

A qualified surveyor ensures accuracy in land size, boundaries, and helps avoid encroachment issues that are common sources of property disputes in Nigeria.

Essential Services:

- **Boundary Survey**: Precise measurement and marking of property boundaries
- **Topographic Survey**: Land elevation and drainage analysis for development planning
- **Building Survey**: Structural assessment of existing buildings

- **Encroachment Detection**: Identification of unauthorized use or boundary violations

Verification Requirements:

- Registration with Surveyors Council of Nigeria (SURCON)
- Experience with your property type and location
- Ability to coordinate with legal team and government offices

Deliverables:

- Current survey plans with official seals and signatures
- Detailed boundary description and coordinate mapping
- Photographic documentation of boundary markers and property condition
- Written reports on any issues or recommendations

4. Builder/Contractor (If Applicable)

For construction or renovation projects, contractor reliability and skill are crucial for project success and cost control.

Qualification Assessment:

- **Corporate Affairs Commission (CAC) registration** for business legitimacy
- **Professional builder association membership** (e.g., Federation of Construction Industry, Association of Professional Builders of Nigeria)
- **Insurance coverage** for liability and performance bonds
- **Bank references** and financial stability verification

Project Management Capabilities:

- Detailed project planning and timeline development
- Materials sourcing and cost management
- Quality control and workmanship standards
- Regular progress reporting and photographic documentation

Performance Agreements:

- Fixed-price contracts with clear scope definitions
- Milestone-based payment schedules tied to completion
- Quality specifications and warranty provisions
- Penalty clauses for delays or substandard work

5. Project Manager

Your project manager serves as your eyes and ears on the ground, monitoring construction, renovations, or property improvements while maintaining regular communication.

Core Responsibilities:

- Daily progress monitoring and photographic documentation
- Quality control and compliance verification
- Coordination between different contractors and professionals
- Budget tracking and expense verification
- Problem identification and resolution recommendations

Communication Requirements:

- Weekly detailed progress reports with photos and financial updates
- Monthly strategic meetings via video conference
- Immediate notification of problems or decisions needed
- Quarterly comprehensive review and planning sessions

Professional Standards:

- Project management certification or extensive experience
- Understanding of Nigerian building codes and regulations
- Strong communication skills and technology proficiency
- Financial management and budget tracking capabilities

6. Property Manager

Especially important for rental properties, property managers handle tenants, maintenance, and rent collection while providing regular performance reports.

Tenant Management Services:

- Tenant screening and selection processes
- Rent collection and deposit management
- Tenant relations and conflict resolution

Property Maintenance:

- Regular inspection schedules and condition reports
- Preventive maintenance planning and execution
- Emergency repair coordination and management
- Vendor management and cost negotiation

Financial Management:

- Monthly income and expense reporting
- Annual budget preparation and variance analysis

7. Accountant

Helps with tracking expenses, ROI calculation, tax planning, and long-term financial strategy optimization. This is especially relevant if you are actively investing in Nigeria and doing so through a registered company or business name because of tax, regulatory and legal compliance.

Financial Services:

- **Expense Tracking**: Detailed recording of all investment-related costs
- **ROI Analysis**: Regular calculation of return on investment and performance metrics
- **Tax Planning**: Optimization of tax obligations in both Nigeria and your country of residence
- **Currency Management**: Strategies for managing exchange rate risk and transfer costs

Reporting Requirements:

- Monthly financial statements with expense categorization
- Quarterly performance analysis and ROI calculations
- Annual tax preparation and compliance documentation
- Strategic planning support for portfolio expansion

Team Building Strategy

Recruitment Process

Phase 1: Research and Identification

- Professional association member directories
- Diaspora investor referral networks
- Online reviews and testimonials where available
- Professional credential verification

Phase 2: Evaluation and Screening

- Initial consultations and capability assessment
- Portfolio review and case study analysis
- Fee structure and service agreement review

Phase 3: Trial Engagement

- Small project or consultation engagement
- Performance evaluation and communication assessment
- Team compatibility and coordination testing
- Long-term engagement decision

Relationship Management

Clear Expectations Setting:

- Written service agreements with specific deliverables
- Communication protocols and reporting schedules
- Performance metrics and accountability measures
- Fee structures and payment terms

Ongoing Management:

- Regular performance reviews and feedback sessions
- Annual service agreement updates and renegotiations
- Professional development support and relationship building
- Team coordination meetings and collaborative planning

Building Accountability Without Micromanagement

Structured Reporting Systems

Regular Reports:

- Progress photos and milestone completion status
- Financial expenditures with receipt documentation
- Problem identification and resolution plans

Monthly Strategic Reviews:

- Performance against established timelines and budgets
- Market updates and opportunity identification
- Risk assessment and mitigation planning
- Strategic adjustments and optimization opportunities

Independent Verification

Third-Party Audits:

- Quarterly independent inspections and progress verification
- Annual financial audits and expense verification
- Professional performance evaluation

Don't assume loyalty based on personal relationships or family connections. Professional competence, clear agreements, and systematic accountability structures ensure successful outcomes regardless of personal relationships.

Team Cost Management

Budget Allocation Guidelines

Professional fees typically represent 10-15% of total project costs:

- Legal services: 3-5% of property value
- Survey services: 1-2% of property value
- Project management: 5-10% of construction costs
- Property management: 8-10% of rental income

Value Optimization Strategies

Long-term Relationships:

- Negotiate better rates for ongoing services
- Bundle services across multiple properties
- Performance bonuses for exceptional results
- Professional development investment for key team members

CTA – Reflect & Act:

Team Assessment Questions:

- Which members of my current team are missing or potentially unreliable?
- What specific qualifications and experience should I prioritize when recruiting team members?
- How will I measure and manage team performance from abroad?
- What systems do I need to implement for effective communication and accountability?

Action Steps:

1. Conduct honest assessment of your current professional team
2. Identify gaps in essential professional services
3. Research and contact qualified professionals in your target investment areas
4. Develop team building timeline and budget allocation

Next Steps: Use the Team Building Template in the workbook to systematically assess, recruit, and manage your professional support system.

Part III

PROTECT WITH POWER

This final section helps you secure your investment for the long term. Learn to manage properties from abroad, avoid post-purchase pitfalls, protect your legal rights, and create a generational legacy.

CHAPTER NINE

MANAGING PROPERTY FROM ABROAD

Investing in Nigerian real estate is only the beginning of your journey—managing your property while living thousands of miles away is where the real challenge lies and where most diaspora investors either succeed spectacularly or fail catastrophically. The difference between these outcomes isn't luck; it's having the right systems, professional partnerships, and processes in place to maintain control and visibility regardless of your physical location.

The Remote Management Reality

Distance Amplifies Everything

When you're managing property from abroad, small problems become large ones quickly, minor miscommunications become major disputes, and simple maintenance issues can become expensive emergencies. The 6-8 hour or more time difference with most diaspora locations means that by the time you wake up to address a problem, an entire business day may have passed in Nigeria.

Common Remote Management Challenges:

- **Communication Delays**: Time zone differences limiting real-time problem-solving
- **Verification Difficulties**: Inability to personally verify claims or inspect work quality
- **Cultural Misunderstandings**: Different business practices and expectation management
- **Financial Control Issues**: Difficulty monitoring expenses and preventing unauthorized costs
- **Emergency Response**: Limited ability to respond quickly to urgent situations

The Cost of Poor Management

Poor remote management doesn't just reduce returns—it can destroy them entirely. A diaspora investor's properties can deteriorate rapidly without proper oversight, tenants can cause damage or stop paying rent without consequences, and contractors can overcharge or perform substandard work.

The Strategic Solution: Professional Property Management

It is a strategic move for you to engage a local property management company, real estate firm, or law firm to represent you and manage your property rather than attempt to manage it yourself. The challenges are enormous and would put a strain on you. However, it is easier for you to manage the firm effectively and for optimal results.

Owning residential or commercial properties has the capacity to generate sustainable income and cash flow if done properly. Property management comes with its own peculiar challenges, but proper management will enable you to maximize the profitability of your real estate investment.

The truth is that property management is not rocket science. The principles are generic and transferable. Even if you are not managing your rental properties yourself, it will serve you in good stead to understand the process and approach it intelligently.

The Foundation: Effective Tenant Selection and Management

Tenant Screening: Your First Line of Defense

As a real estate investor, one of the most important aspects of rental property success is tenant selection. This can be a blessing or a pain depending on the type of tenants occupying your property. When you have a good tenant who pays rent regularly, maintains the property well, and relates well with neighbors, this investment becomes a blessing. However, a tenant that defaults frequently in rent payment and is problematic can make this investment a nightmare.

Essential Tenant Screening Process:

Application Requirements: Have a standard questionnaire that every prospective tenant must complete, including:

- Why they are moving from their current accommodation
- How many people will be living in the property
- Employment details and income verification
- References from employers, former landlords, or neutral third parties

Red Flag Indicators:

- Tenants who were evicted or are suing their former landlord
- Excessive urgency or desperation to secure the property immediately
- Inability to provide specific details about their business or employment
- Requests for rent concessions or inability to pay security deposits
- Unwillingness to pay professional fees for the transaction

Financial Capability Assessment: Generally, it is better to rent your property to those working in relatively well-known companies or established professionals. Be cautious of those who say they are doing business without going into specifics about their goods or services. Based on their income information and family size, you should be able to reasonably project whether they can pay rent regularly.

Due Diligence Requirements: Once a tenant scales through preliminary screening, go a step further to do reference checks and confirm they are working or doing business where they stated. If you find this information is incorrect, do not rent your property to them regardless of how much they're willing to pay.

Establishing Clear Tenant Management Frameworks

Lease Agreement Essentials:

- Detailed terms covering rent amounts, payment dates, and late payment penalties
- Clear maintenance responsibilities for both landlord and tenant
- Specific payment methods and procedures
- Property condition requirements and inspection schedules
- Rules for property use and tenant behavior

Tenant Responsibilities: A tenant is expected to:

- Pay rent regularly and on time
- Hand over the property in decent condition (excluding reasonable wear and tear)
- Pay for utilities being used (electricity, water, etc.)
- Maintain peaceful coexistence with other tenants
- Avoid illegal activities or anything constituting a nuisance
- Obtain landlord consent before making any major modifications

Professional Service Agreements and Accountability

Clear, detailed contracts eliminate ambiguity and provide legal recourse when problems arise. Every relationship in your property management ecosystem should be governed by written agreements with specific performance standards.

Property Manager Service Agreements

Specific Deliverables:

- Monthly financial reports with all income and expenses
- Quarterly comprehensive property inspections
- Annual maintenance schedules and budget planning

- Immediate emergency response and communication

Performance Metrics:

- Response times for emergencies
- Tenant satisfaction maintenance and retention rates
- Financial reporting accuracy and timeliness
- Property condition maintenance standards

Communication Protocols:

- Regular updates on property status and any issues
- Video calls for strategic discussions
- Quarterly comprehensive reviews and planning sessions
- Immediate notification of any emergencies or significant issues

Accountability Measures:

- Performance bonuses for excellent service
- Penalty clauses for poor performance or delays
- Clear termination conditions and procedures
- Regular performance evaluations and feedback

Maintenance and Repair Management

A critical element of effective property management is ensuring prompt response to maintenance issues. Many landlords forget this rule and push all forms of repairs to tenants, which is counterproductive since tenants are not motivated to maintain the property to the highest standard possible.

Maintenance Philosophy: Your property is an investment that requires proper maintenance. This requires scheduled inspections and addressing issues promptly. When you postpone necessary repairs, the damage often costs more later. There is a direct correlation between property condition and the rent it can command—well-maintained properties generally command higher rent and enjoy lower vacancy rates.

Maintenance Categories:

- **Major Repairs**: Landlord's responsibility (structural, plumbing, electrical systems)
- **Minor Maintenance**: Often tenant responsibility (light bulbs, basic cleaning)
- **Preventive Maintenance**: Scheduled upkeep to prevent major problems
- **Emergency Repairs**: Immediate response required regardless of cost

Financial Management and Rent Collection

Rent Collection and Management

One of the critical aspects of property management is rent collection and rent increment. Most real estate investors assume they can increase rent whenever they want, but there are legal restrictions and standard practices to follow.

Rent Management Best Practices:

- After initial rent payment, allow at least one year before first rent review
- Provide sufficient notice before implementing any rent increases (typically 3-6 months)
- Rent increases should be reasonable and in line with market rates
- Maintain detailed records of all rent payments and communications

Payment Procedures:

- Establish clear payment methods and due dates
- Implement late payment penalties consistently
- Maintain detailed records of all payments received
- Follow up promptly on any missed payments

Record Keeping and Documentation

Good property management always involves reasonable paperwork and record keeping. You need to write to tenants about late payments or maintenance issues. Keep detailed inspection reports and all receipts. These management requirements can be burdensome for those not suited for such challenges or who cannot spare time for such actions.

Essential Records:

- All tenant communications and notices
- Maintenance requests and completion records
- Financial transactions and receipts
- Property inspection reports
- Insurance and legal documents

Understanding Landlord-Tenant Legal Framework

The relationship between landlords and tenants is one of the most intricate in Nigeria. A basic understanding of legal principles is essential knowledge for any real estate investor.

Landlord Responsibilities

The landlord is not just a rent collector. Key responsibilities include:

- Keeping premises in habitable condition
- Ensuring tenants can live peacefully without landlord or agents causing nuisance
- Maintaining compliance with tenancy agreement terms
- Handling major repairs and structural maintenance
- Paying property-related government charges (like Land Use Charge)

Tenant Obligations

Anyone occupying premises (whether paying rent or not) is considered a tenant unless claiming ownership. Tenant obligations include:

- Regular and timely rent payment
- Reasonable care of the property
- Payment for utilities consumed
- Peaceful coexistence with other tenants
- Compliance with property rules and legal requirements

Ending Tenancy Relationships

The relationship between landlord and tenant can be ended willingly, unilaterally, or by law. When a landlord decides to end the relationship, proper legal process must be followed:

- Appropriate notice to quit must be given
- Due process of law must be complied with
- Legal assistance may be required for complex situations
- Physical removal of tenant property without legal process is illegal

Regular Audits and Independent Verification

Surprise inspections and independent audits are essential for maintaining accountability and identifying problems before they become expensive disasters.

Quarterly Property Inspections

- **Independent Inspectors**: Use professionals not connected to your regular management team
- **Comprehensive Checklists**: Standardized inspection forms covering all property systems
- **Photographic Documentation**: Before and after photos of all property areas
- **Condition Reports**: Detailed written assessments with recommendations for action

Financial Audits

- **Expense Verification**: Independent review of all claimed expenses with receipt verification
- **Rent Collection Audits**: Verification of tenant payments and deposit management
- **Maintenance Cost Analysis**: Comparison of costs against market rates and quality standards
- **Budget Variance Reports**: Analysis of actual versus projected expenses with explanations

Choosing the Right Management Approach

The level of maintenance and management you give to a property should be based on your medium or long-term goals. If you purchased property solely to sell within a few months due to rising values, you may consider major renovation works unnecessary.

However, for long-term rental properties, consistent maintenance and professional management are essential for:

- Maximizing rental income potential
- Maintaining and increasing property value
- Minimizing vacancy periods
- Protecting your investment from deterioration
- Ensuring compliance with all legal requirements

If you cannot spare time for detailed management or lack the expertise for handling tenant relations, maintenance coordination, and financial management, it is better to appoint a professional property management company to handle the details.

Building Your Management Success Framework

Successful remote property management requires:

- **Professional Team**: Qualified property managers, lawyers, and maintenance providers
- **Clear Systems**: Written agreements, reporting schedules, and accountability measures
- **Regular Oversight**: Scheduled inspections, audits, and performance reviews
- **Legal Compliance**: Understanding and following landlord-tenant laws
- **Financial Controls**: Detailed record keeping and expense management
- **Long-term Perspective**: Viewing management as investment in property value and returns

Remember: effective property management is not about micromanaging from abroad—it's about establishing systems and relationships that work reliably in your absence while providing you with the oversight and control necessary to protect and grow your investment.

CTA – Reflect & Act:

Management System Assessment:

- What management tools am I currently using, and what critical gaps exist in my systems?
- How effectively can I verify the claims and reports I receive from my local team?
- What would happen to my properties if my primary contact person became unavailable?
- Do I have adequate tenant screening and management procedures in place?

Action Steps:

1. Evaluate your current property management systems against best practices outlined in this chapter
2. Identify qualified property management professionals or companies in your target areas
3. Create or update service agreements with all members of your property management team
4. Establish regular audit and verification procedures to ensure accountability

Next Steps: Use the Remote Management Checklist in the workbook to systematically assess and strengthen your property management systems. Focus on building professional relationships and clear systems rather than trying to manage every detail from abroad.

CHAPTER TEN

YOUR NEXT STEP – SECURE YOUR LEGACY

The true value of real estate investment extends far beyond immediate profit—it lies in the legacy you create for future generations and the lasting impact of your strategic financial decisions. Your property investment journey doesn't end when the purchase is complete or when the building is constructed; it continues through how your assets are managed, protected, transferred, and multiplied over time.

For diaspora Nigerians, legacy planning carries additional complexity due to cross-border asset ownership, different legal systems, and the unique challenges of managing inheritance across multiple jurisdictions. However, with proper planning, your Nigerian property investments can become a cornerstone of generational wealth that benefits your family for decades to come.

Understanding Legacy in Property Investment

Beyond Personal Wealth

Legacy building transforms property investment from a personal financial strategy into a multi-generational wealth creation system. Your properties in Nigeria can provide financial security for your children, educational funding for grandchildren, and a tangible connection to their Nigerian heritage regardless of where they live.

Legacy Components:

- **Financial Legacy**: The monetary value and income generation from your properties
- **Educational Legacy**: The knowledge and skills you transfer about property investment
- **Cultural Legacy**: The connection to Nigeria and family heritage through property ownership
- **Social Legacy**: The positive impact your investments have on local communities

The Power of Compound Growth

Property that appreciates at 8-12% annually (typical for well-selected Nigerian real estate) can multiply in value dramatically over generations. A property worth N50 million today could be worth N400-800 million in your grandchildren's lifetime, providing financial foundation for education, business ventures, and continued investment.

How to Turn Property into Legacy

1. Estate Planning: The Foundation of Legacy

Estate planning for diaspora investors requires navigating both Nigerian and international legal systems to ensure your wishes are honored and your beneficiaries are protected.

Will Creation for Nigerian Assets: In Nigeria, a will is a testamentary document that expresses a person's last wishes as to how their property is to be distributed after death. The testator must be of legal age and sound mind, with the will properly witnessed and executed according to Nigerian law.

Essential Will Components:

- **Full identification** of the testator including name, address, and occupation
- **Complete asset inventory** including all Nigerian properties with detailed descriptions
- **Clear beneficiary designation** with full names and addresses of all inheritors
- **Executor appointment** specifying who will manage the estate distribution
- **Guardian designation** for minor children if applicable
- **Specific bequests** detailing exactly which assets go to which beneficiaries

Trust Structures for Complex Estates: Nigerian law recognizes both living trusts (created during your lifetime) and testamentary trusts (created through your will). Trusts offer several advantages over simple wills, including faster distribution (avoiding probate), greater privacy, and ongoing management for minor beneficiaries.

Trust Benefits for Diaspora Investors:

- **Probate Avoidance**: Trusts pass outside of probate, saving time and money
- **Professional Management**: Trustee can manage properties until beneficiaries are ready
- **Tax Optimization**: Proper trust structure can minimize estate taxes
- **Privacy Protection**: Trust distributions are private unlike probate proceedings
- **Continued Income**: Beneficiaries can receive ongoing income while preserving principal

Cross-Border Considerations: Estate planning for diaspora investors must consider both Nigerian inheritance law and the laws of your country of residence. Some countries have estate taxes that could affect your Nigerian assets, while Nigeria has its own succession laws that must be followed.

2. Documentation: The Cornerstone of Security

Comprehensive documentation ensures your heirs can access and manage your Nigerian properties without legal complications or unnecessary delays.

Essential Document Categories:

Title Documents:

- **Original Certificates of Occupancy** with all registration stamps and seals
- **Deeds of Assignment** showing clear chain of title from original allocation
- **Survey Plans** with registered surveyor certifications and boundary descriptions
- **Governor's Consent** documents for all transfers requiring government approval

Financial Records:

- **Purchase documentation** showing all payments made and methods of funding
- **Improvement records** documenting all renovations, constructions, and upgrades
- **Insurance policies** covering property damage, title issues, and liability
- **Tax records** showing property tax payments and compliance with all obligations

Management Documentation:

- **Property management agreements** with contact information for all service providers
- **Tenant leases and rental history** for income-producing properties
- **Maintenance contracts** for ongoing property upkeep and improvements
- **Bank account information** for properties including local Nigerian accounts

Digital Documentation Strategy: Create comprehensive digital archives that can be accessed by your heirs from anywhere in the world:

Cloud Storage Systems:

- **Secure cloud platforms** with multiple backup locations and encryption
- **Organized folder structures** making it easy to locate specific documents
- **Access control systems** allowing different levels of access for different family members
- **Regular backup procedures** ensuring no documents are ever lost

Physical Document Security: Maintain original documents in secure, accessible locations with copies distributed to trusted individuals in multiple countries.

3. Education: Empowering the Next Generation

The most valuable legacy you can create is knowledge—teaching your family how to continue building and managing property investments successfully.

Financial Education Components:

- **Real Estate Fundamentals**: Basic principles of property investment and management

- **Nigerian Market Knowledge**: Specific insights about local markets, regulations, and opportunities
- **Cross-border Finance**: Understanding currency management, international banking, and tax implications
- **Risk Management**: How to evaluate and mitigate investment risks effectively

Practical Involvement Strategies:

- **Include family members** in property decisions and management discussions
- **Share investment analysis** showing how you evaluate potential opportunities
- **Involve them in property visits** during trips to Nigeria so they understand the assets firsthand
- **Create learning opportunities** through real estate seminars, courses, and networking events

Succession Planning: Prepare family members to take increasing responsibility for property management:

- **Gradual responsibility transfer** starting with small decisions and expanding over time
- **Mentorship programs** pairing younger family members with experienced investors
- **Professional development** supporting family members who want to develop real estate expertise
- **Network introduction** connecting family members with your professional team in Nigeria

4. Reinvestment: Multiplying Your Legacy

Strategic reinvestment of rental income and property appreciation can exponentially increase the value of your legacy over time.

Reinvestment Strategies:

- **Property Expansion**: Use rental income to purchase additional properties in high-growth areas
- **Property Improvement**: Reinvest in upgrades that increase value and rental income potential
- **Diversification**: Expand into different property types and locations to reduce risk
- **Education Investment**: Use property income to fund family education and professional development

5. Insurance: Protecting Your Legacy

Comprehensive insurance protection ensures your legacy survives unexpected events that could otherwise destroy decades of careful building.

Making It Official: Implementation Strategy

1. Create Comprehensive Property Folders

Physical Property Folder:

- **Master binder** with all original documents for each property
- **Property summary sheets** with key information for each asset
- **Contact information** for all professionals involved with each property
- **Instructions** for accessing digital files and online accounts

Digital Property Archive:

- **Secure cloud storage** with organized folders for each property
- **Digital copies** of all physical documents with high-resolution scanning
- **Video documentation** of each property's condition and important features

- **Financial spreadsheets** tracking all income, expenses, and performance metrics

2. Annual Portfolio Reviews

Financial Performance Analysis:

- **Return on investment** calculations for each property
- **Cash flow analysis** showing income, expenses, and net returns
- **Market value assessments** based on comparable sales and professional appraisals
- **Portfolio diversification** review ensuring appropriate risk distribution

Strategic Planning Updates:

- **Market opportunity assessment** for potential new investments
- **Property improvement planning** for value enhancement projects
- **Family involvement evaluation** assessing readiness for increased responsibility
- **Estate plan updates** reflecting any changes in circumstances or laws

3. Professional Legacy Team Assembly

Estate Planning Professionals:

- **Estate attorney** specializing in cross-border asset management
- **Tax advisor** understanding both Nigerian and international tax implications
- **Financial planner** with expertise in generational wealth building
- **Trust administrator** for ongoing trust management if applicable

Property Management Team:

- **Nigerian property lawyer** for ongoing legal compliance and documentation

- **Property manager** with proven track record and family relationship capability
- **Financial advisor** in Nigeria for local banking and investment opportunities
- **Insurance agent** providing comprehensive coverage and claims support

4. Legacy Success Measurement

Quantitative Metrics:

- **Portfolio Value Growth**: Annual appreciation rates and total value increase
- **Income Generation**: Rental yield improvement and cash flow sustainability
- **Family Participation**: Number of family members actively involved in property decisions
- **Knowledge Transfer**: Family members' demonstrated understanding of property investment

Qualitative Indicators:

- **Family Unity**: Property investments strengthening rather than dividing family relationships
- **Cultural Connection**: Younger generations maintaining ties to Nigeria through property ownership
- **Professional Relationships**: Strong, ongoing relationships with Nigerian professional team
- **Community Impact**: Positive contribution to Nigerian communities through responsible property investment

The Continuous Legacy Journey

Legacy building is not a one-time event but an ongoing process that evolves as your family grows, circumstances change, and new opportunities arise. Your Nigerian property investments can become the foundation for a multi-generational wealth-building system that provides financial security, cultural connection, and educational opportunities for your descendants.

The key is starting now, regardless of your current portfolio size or family situation. Every property properly acquired, documented, and managed becomes part of your legacy. Every family member educated about property investment becomes a potential steward of that legacy. Every system you implement to protect and grow your assets contributes to long-term success.

Your legacy is not just about the properties you own today—it's about the foundation you're building for generations of prosperity, opportunity, and connection to Nigeria.

CTA – Reflect & Act:

Legacy Planning Assessment:

- What happens to my Nigerian properties if something happens to me tomorrow?
- Do my family members understand the value and potential of my property investments?
- Are my important documents accessible to my heirs and properly organized?
- How am I currently reinvesting property income to multiply my legacy over time?

Immediate Action Steps:

1. Conduct comprehensive inventory of all property-related documents and identify gaps
2. Schedule consultation with estate planning attorney familiar with Nigerian assets
3. Create digital archive system for all property documentation and begin systematic organization
4. Involve family members in next property review or investment decision

Long-term Planning:

- **Within 30 days**: Complete initial documentation audit and begin digital archiving
- **Within 90 days**: Meet with estate planning attorney and draft or update will including Nigerian assets
- **Within 6 months**: Implement comprehensive insurance coverage and establish trust if appropriate
- **Within 12 months**: Conduct first annual portfolio review with family members and establish ongoing education program

Next Steps: Use the Legacy Builder Toolkit in the workbook to systematically implement your estate planning and legacy creation strategy. This comprehensive toolkit includes document checklists, family education templates, reinvestment calculators, and annual review frameworks specifically designed for diaspora property investors building generational wealth through Nigerian real estate.

CHAPTER ELEVEN

YOUR PROPERTY ACTION PLAN

Congratulations! You've now completed your journey through the Diaspora Property Formula. You've learned about market opportunities, avoided critical traps, understood legal requirements, and assembled professional teams. But knowledge without action brings no change to your life or financial situation.

This concluding chapter is designed to transform your understanding into a practical, personalized action plan that moves you from knowledge to ownership, from planning to profit, and from dreaming about Nigerian property investment to building wealth through strategic real estate acquisition.

The time for analysis is ending. The time for action is now.

From Information to Implementation

The Knowledge-Action Gap

Most people who read books about real estate investment never actually buy a single property. They become educated observers rather than active participants. The difference between those who succeed and those who remain on the sidelines isn't intelligence or resources—it's the willingness to take systematic, well-planned action despite uncertainty and risk.

Your Nigerian property investment journey requires moving from theoretical understanding to practical implementation. This means making real decisions with real money, building actual relationships with Nigerian professionals, and taking tangible steps toward property ownership.

The Power of Systematic Implementation

Random action leads to random results. Systematic action based on proven frameworks leads to predictable success. The Diaspora Property Formula provides the systematic approach, but you must provide the implementation discipline.

Why Systematic Implementation Works:

- Reduces decision fatigue by providing clear next steps.
- Minimizes costly mistakes through proven processes.
- Creates accountability through measurable milestones.
- Builds confidence through incremental progress.
- Prevents vital details from being missed.

Step-by-Step Implementation Roadmap

Step 1: Set Your Goal – Define Success Specifically

Vague goals produce vague results. "I want to invest in Nigerian property" is not a goal—it's a wish. Your implementation must begin with crystal-clear, specific, measurable objectives.

Goal Definition Framework:

Financial Objectives:

- Specific investment amount (e.g., "$75,000 over 18 months")
- Target return expectations (e.g., "15% annual ROI including rental income")
- Timeline for investment recovery (e.g., "Break Even within 7 years")
- Income generation goals (e.g., "$800 monthly rental income by year 3")

Property Specifications:

- Property type (land, residential, commercial, mixed-use)
- Size requirements (square meters, number of rooms, lot size)
- Development intentions (immediate construction, future development, land banking)
- Usage plans (personal residence, rental property, family compound)

Personal Motivations:

- Legacy creation objectives (generational wealth, family heritage)
- Cultural connection goals (maintaining Nigeria ties, family visits)
- Retirement planning (future relocation, income security)
- Investment diversification (portfolio expansion, currency hedging)

Example Goal Statement: "Within 24 months, I will purchase 2-3 residential plots totaling 1,800 square meters in a growth corridor within 30 km of Lagos or Abuja, with clean Certificate of Occupancy documentation, for a total investment of $60,000-80,000, to begin construction of rental properties that will generate $1,000+ monthly income by year 4."

Step 2: Pick a Location – Apply Strategic Selection Criteria

Location selection should be based on objective analysis rather than emotional attachment or family recommendations. Use the criteria learned in Chapters 3 and 7 to make data-driven decisions.

Location Selection Process:

Primary Research Phase:

- Identify 5-7 potential areas based on infrastructure development plans.
- Research government investment announcements and budget allocations.
- Analyze population growth and urbanization trends in target areas.
- Evaluate transportation development and access improvements.

Comparative Analysis:

- Create location scorecard for each potential area (Chapter 7 methodology)
- Compare current prices versus projected appreciation potential.
- Assess rental demand and yield expectations for each location.
- Evaluate risk factors including security, flooding, and legal clarity.

Professional Verification:

- Engage local real estate professionals for market insights.
- Conduct independent research through multiple sources.
- Verify infrastructure development timelines and funding status.
- Confirm legal and regulatory compliance in target areas.

Decision Matrix: Create a weighted scoring system based on your priorities:

- Infrastructure development (25%)
- Appreciation potential (25%)
- Rental income opportunity (20%)
- Legal and regulatory clarity (15%)
- Personal accessibility and comfort (15%)

Step 3: Define Your Budget – Include All Investment Components

Most diaspora investors underestimate total investment requirements by focusing only on property purchase prices. Comprehensive budget planning prevents financial surprises and ensures adequate reserves for unexpected costs.

Complete Investment Budget Components:

Property Acquisition (60-70% of total budget):

- Property purchase price
- Agent commissions (typically 5-10% of property value)
- Currency conversion costs and transfer fees

Legal and Documentation (8-12% of total budget):

- Legal fees for title search and verification
- Survey costs for boundary confirmation
- Government registration and stamp duty fees
- Governor's consent fees if required

Development and Improvement (varies based on plans):

- Construction costs if building immediately
- Site preparation and infrastructure connection
- Architectural and engineering fees
- Building permits and approval costs

Professional Services (3-5% of total budget):

- Property management setup fees
- Insurance premiums and coverage costs
- Ongoing professional service retainers

Contingency Reserves (15-20% of total budget):

- Emergency fund for unexpected costs
- Currency fluctuation buffer
- Construction cost overrun reserves
- Legal dispute or complication funds

Sample Budget Breakdown ($75,000 total investment):

- Property purchase: $52,500 (70%)
- Legal and documentation: $7,500 (10%)
- Professional services: $3,750 (5%)
- Contingency reserves: $11,250 (15%)

Step 4: Assemble Your Team – Build Professional Relationships

Your success depends entirely on the quality of professionals you engage. Team assembly should be systematic and thorough rather than rushed or based on convenience.

Team Assembly Process:

Phase 1: Research and Identification (Weeks 1-4)

- Research professional associations and member directories
- Collect referrals from multiple diaspora investor sources
- Create initial contact list of 3-5 candidates for each role
- Verify professional credentials and licensing status

Phase 2: Evaluation and Screening (Weeks 5-8)

- Conduct initial consultations with all candidates
- Compare fee structures and service offerings
- Assess communication style and diaspora experience

Phase 3: Selection and Engagement (Weeks 9-12)

- Select preferred professional for each role
- Negotiate service agreements and fee structures
- Establish communication protocols and reporting schedules
- Begin working relationships with small initial engagements

Essential Team Members Priority Order:

1. **Real Estate Lawyer** (highest priority - needed for all transactions)
2. **Licensed Surveyor** (critical for property verification)
3. **Real Estate Agent/Consultant** (important for deal flow and negotiation)
4. **Property Manager** (essential for ongoing oversight)

5. **Accountant/Financial Advisor** (valuable for tax and performance tracking)

Step 5: Use the Workbook – Complete Implementation Templates

The DPF Workbook provides systematic templates that transform the frameworks in this book into practical tools for your specific situation. Complete implementation requires using these tools consistently.

Critical Workbook Components:

Investment Planning Templates:

- Goal definition and timeline worksheet
- Budget planning and cash flow projection
- Location selection and scoring matrix
- Risk assessment and mitigation planning

Due Diligence Checklists:

- Property verification and documentation review
- Professional team evaluation and selection
- Legal and regulatory compliance confirmation
- Financial analysis and return calculation

Ongoing Management Tools:

- Communication and reporting schedules
- Performance tracking and milestone monitoring
- Problem identification and resolution procedures
- Annual review and strategic planning frameworks

Progress Tracking Systems:

- Monthly action item completion checklists
- Quarterly goal progress assessment
- Annual portfolio review and optimization
- Multi-year strategic planning updates

Step 6: Take Your First Step – Begin Implementation Immediately

The most crucial step is the first one. Momentum builds through action, not planning. Your first step should be specific, achievable, and scheduled for completion within the next 7 days.

First Step Options (Choose One for This Week):

Option 1: Professional Consultation

- Schedule consultation with Nigerian real estate lawyer
- Prepare list of questions about investment process and requirements
- Discuss your investment goals and timeline
- Request referrals for other professional team members

Option 2: Market Research Launch

- Begin systematic research on your top 3 target locations
- Create spreadsheet to track property prices and development news
- Search using dedicated Nigerian real estate portals
- Join diaspora investor communities and online forums

Option 3: Financial Preparation

- Open domiciliary account with Nigerian bank for property transactions
- Research currency transfer options and costs
- Establish investment budget and savings plan
- Begin setting aside monthly funds for property investment

Option 4: Property Scouting

- Contact reputable real estate agencies in target areas
- Request property listings that match your criteria and budget
- Schedule virtual property tours for promising opportunities
- Begin building relationships with potential agents and consultants

Implementation Timeline and Milestones

1. 30-Day Sprint (Month 1):

Week 1:

- Complete goal definition and write specific investment objectives
- Begin location research and create initial target list
- Make first professional contact (lawyer or real estate consultant)

Week 2:

- Establish complete investment budget including all cost categories
- Research and contact 3-5 potential team members for each role
- Begin systematic market research on top target locations

Week 3:

- Conduct first professional consultations and interviews
- Complete location scoring and begin narrowing target areas
- Set up financial systems for international property investment

Week 4:

- Finalize professional team selection and begin formal engagements
- Choose final target location based on research and analysis
- Create detailed action plan for next 90 days

2. 90-Day Foundation Building (Months 2-4):

Month 2:

- Complete all professional team assembly and service agreements
- Conduct comprehensive market research and property identification
- Begin serious property evaluation and due diligence processes

Month 3:

- Identify and evaluate specific property opportunities
- Conduct detailed financial analysis and return projections
- Negotiate preliminary terms for most promising opportunities

Month 4:

- Complete final due diligence and property verification

- Finalize purchase negotiations and legal documentation
- Execute property acquisition or commit to development timeline

3. 12-Month Completion Cycle (Year 1):

- Property acquisition and legal completion
- Development planning and execution if applicable
- Team optimization and relationship refinement
- Performance monitoring and strategic adjustment

Accountability and Progress Tracking

Weekly Progress Reviews:

Every Sunday, spend 30 minutes reviewing the past week's progress and planning the coming week's priorities. Use these questions:

- What specific actions did I complete toward my property investment goals?
- What obstacles or challenges did I encounter, and how did I address them?
- What are my three most important tasks for the coming week?
- What support or resources do I need to maintain momentum?

Monthly Strategic Assessments:

On the last day of each month, conduct a comprehensive review:

- Am I on track to meet my timeline and milestone commitments?
- **What should I change in my strategy or approach?**
- How effectively are my professional team members performing?
- What new opportunities or challenges have emerged that require attention?

Quarterly Deep Dives:

Every three months, step back for strategic planning:

- Comprehensive goal progress assessment and timeline adjustment

- Market condition changes and impact on investment strategy
- Professional relationship evaluation and optimization
- Financial performance analysis and budget reallocation if needed

Maintaining Momentum Despite Challenges

Common Implementation Obstacles:

Analysis Paralysis:

- Solution: Set decision deadlines and commit to taking action based on available information
- Remember: Perfect information doesn't exist, but systematic analysis reduces risk adequately

Overwhelm from Complexity:

- Solution: Focus on one step at a time rather than trying to manage everything simultaneously
- Use the DPF framework to maintain systematic progress through complexity

Distance and Communication Challenges:

- Solution: Establish regular communication schedules and use technology effectively
- Over-communicate rather than under-communicate with your Nigerian team

Financial Concerns and Currency Fluctuations:

- Solution: Build adequate reserves and use professional financial planning
- Focus on long-term wealth building rather than short-term currency movements

Success Maintenance Strategies:

Celebrate Milestones: Acknowledge and celebrate progress at each major milestone to maintain motivation and momentum.

Learn Continuously: Stay informed about Nigerian real estate markets, regulations, and opportunities through ongoing education.

Network Actively: Build relationships with other diaspora investors and learn from their experiences and insights.

Adapt Systematically: Use the DPF framework to adapt your approach based on changing circumstances while maintaining strategic focus.

Your 90-Day Commitment

Print out your personalized roadmap and post it where you'll see it daily. Make a public commitment to yourself and your family about your Nigerian property investment goals. Schedule a 90-day progress review appointment in your calendar right now.

Most importantly, commit to taking one specific action every week for the next 90 days. Small, consistent actions compound into major achievements over time.

The Beginning of Your Legacy

This book ends, but your property investment journey begins now. The Diaspora Property Formula provides the roadmap, but your commitment to systematic implementation determines your success.

Nigerian real estate represents one of the world's most dynamic investment opportunities, driven by population growth, urbanization, and economic development. For diaspora investors with foreign currency advantages and systematic approaches, the potential for wealth creation is extraordinary.

Your Nigerian property investment can become the foundation for generational wealth, cultural connection, and personal fulfillment. The knowledge you've gained through this book, combined with systematic action through your personalized plan, can transform your financial future and create legacy for your family.

The question is not whether Nigerian property investment can succeed for diaspora investors—the evidence clearly demonstrates it can. The question is whether you will take the systematic action required to join the ranks of successful diaspora property investors.

Your action plan is complete. Your roadmap is clear. Your next step is waiting.

The time to begin is now.

Final CTA – Reflect & Act:

Commitment Questions:

- What is the ONE thing I will do this week to begin implementing the Diaspora Property Formula?
- What specific milestone will I achieve in the next 90 days to advance my property investment goals?
- Who will I tell about my investment plans to create accountability for my success?
- When will I schedule my first 90-day progress review to assess my implementation progress?

Immediate Action Steps:

1. **Today**: Write your specific investment goal using the framework provided in Step 1
2. **This Week**: Take your chosen first step from Step 6 options
3. **This Month**: Complete your 30-day sprint milestones
4. **Next 90 Days**: Execute your foundation building plan systematically

Resource Access:

- Go to www.diasporapropertyformula.com/workbook to download your free DPF Workbook
- Access implementation templates, checklists, and tracking tools
- Join the diaspora investor community for ongoing support and networking
- Schedule optional consultation for personalized implementation guidance

Your Property Investment Journey Starts Now

The knowledge is complete. The tools are available. The opportunities are waiting.

Your success depends entirely on your willingness to take systematic, consistent action based on the proven framework you've learned.

Begin today. Your future self will thank you.

THANK YOU FOR COMPLETING THIS JOURNEY

Congratulations! You've now equipped yourself with the Diaspora Property Formula™—a proven system developed through two decades of successful property investment across Nigeria and Australia.

You now have the knowledge to avoid the costly mistakes that destroy most diaspora property investments. But knowledge without action remains just potential.

To help you implement everything you've learned immediately, I've created a comprehensive companion workbook with all the tools, templates, and assessments you need to turn the Diaspora Property Formula™ into your personal wealth-building system.

Your Complete Investment Toolkit Includes:

- **Investment Readiness Assessment** - Determine your optimal investment strategy
- **Market Intelligence Tracker** - Stay ahead of property market trends
- **5-Point Location Scorecard** - Evaluate any Nigerian location for investment potential
- **Professional Team Building Templates** - Find and manage trusted partners

- **Legal Due Diligence Checklist** - Protect yourself from fraud and legal issues
- **Property Acquisition Worksheet** - Step-by-step transaction management
- **Risk Assessment Framework** - Minimize investment risks
- **Currency Optimization Calculator** - Maximize your foreign exchange advantage
- **Remote Management System** - Oversee your properties from anywhere
- **Wealth Building Tracker** - Monitor and grow your property portfolio

Download Your Free Workbook

This comprehensive workbook is my gift to you—everything you need to implement the Diaspora Property Formula™ successfully and safely.

www.diasporapropertyformula.com/workbook

Transform your property investment dreams into wealth-building reality with the proven systems inside your Diaspora Property Formula Workbook.

GLOSSARY OF TERMS

A

Agent Commission - Fee paid to real estate agents, typically 5-10% of property value in Nigeria, for facilitating property transactions.

Appreciation - The increase in property value over time due to market forces, improvements, or development in the surrounding area.

Assignment, Deed of - Legal document that transfers ownership of property from seller to buyer, must be properly executed and registered.

B

Boundary Survey - Professional measurement and marking of property boundaries to prevent disputes and confirm exact property dimensions.

Building Approval - Government permission required before construction can begin, ensuring compliance with local building codes and zoning regulations.

Buy and Hold Strategy - Investment approach focusing on purchasing property for long-term appreciation rather than immediate resale.

C

Certificate of Occupancy (C of O) - Government-issued document confirming legal right to occupy and use land, the strongest form of property title in Nigeria.

Chain of Title - Complete history of property ownership from original government allocation to current owner, essential for verification.

Customary Land - Land governed by traditional/customary law rather than statutory law, often family or community-owned.

Currency Hedging - Financial strategy to protect against exchange rate fluctuations when investing across different currencies.

D

Diaspora - Nigerians living outside Nigeria, particularly those in developed countries with stronger currencies.

Domiciliary Account - Bank account in Nigeria that holds foreign currency (USD, GBP, EUR), useful for property transactions.

Due Diligence - Comprehensive investigation and verification process before purchasing property to identify potential risks or problems.

Developer Payment Plan - Structured payment schedule offered by property developers, typically spread over 6-24 months.

E

Encroachment - Unauthorized use or occupation of part of a property by neighbors or third parties.

Escrow - Third-party service that holds funds until specific conditions are met, providing security for both buyer and seller.

Estate Planning - Process of arranging for the transfer of property and assets after death, including wills and trusts.

Excision - Government process of removing land from customary ownership and converting it to statutory ownership with proper titles.

F

FMBN - Federal Mortgage Bank of Nigeria, government institution providing mortgage financing including diaspora-specific programs.

Family Land - Property owned collectively by extended family under customary law, often source of ownership disputes.

G

Governor's Consent - Mandatory government approval required when transferring property with Certificate of Occupancy, typically takes 6-18 months.

Growth Corridor - Geographic area experiencing rapid development due to infrastructure projects or economic activity.

Gazette - Official government publication announcing land acquisitions, planning changes, and other legal notices.

H

Housing Deficit - Shortage of adequate housing units relative to population demand, estimated at over 17 million units in Nigeria.

I

Infrastructure Development - Construction of roads, utilities, airports, ports, and other facilities that increase property values.

Investment Yield - Annual return on investment, calculated as annual rental income divided by property value.

L

Land Banking - Strategy of purchasing undeveloped land for future appreciation as surrounding areas develop.

Land Registry - Government office where property titles and transfers are officially recorded and can be verified.

Land Use Act 1978 - Nigerian law that vests all land ownership in state governments, forming basis of current property law.

Land Use Charge - Annual property tax paid to state governments, typically responsibility of property owner.

Lien - Legal claim against property, often for unpaid debts, that must be resolved before clean transfer of ownership.

M

Market Appreciation - Rate at which property values increase over time in a specific location or market.

Milestone Payments - Payment schedule tied to specific project completion stages rather than time periods.

Mortgage - Loan secured by property, with typical terms in Nigeria of 10-15 years at double-digit interest rates.

N

NHF - National Housing Fund, government program offering low-interest loans for property purchase, including diaspora schemes.

NIESV - Nigerian Institution of Estate Surveyors and Valuers, professional body regulating real estate professionals.

O

Off-plan Purchase - Buying property before construction is completed, often at lower prices but with higher risks.

P

Property Management - Professional service handling day-to-day operations of rental properties including tenant relations and maintenance.

Probate - Court-supervised process of validating wills and distributing deceased person's assets.

R

REDAN - Real Estate Developers Association of Nigeria, professional body for property developers.

Rental Yield - Annual rental income as percentage of property value, key metric for investment properties.

Right of Occupancy - Legal right to use land, can be customary (traditional) or statutory (government-granted).

S

Statutory Right of Occupancy - Government-granted right to occupy land, provides stronger legal protection than customary rights.

Survey Plan - Technical drawing showing exact property boundaries, dimensions, and coordinates, prepared by licensed surveyor.

SURCON - Surveyors Council of Nigeria, regulatory body for professional surveyors.

Stamp Duty - Government tax on legal documents including property transfers, must be paid for valid documentation.

T

Title Search - Investigation of property ownership history to verify legitimate ownership and identify potential problems.

Title Verification - Process of confirming authenticity and validity of property documents through official channels.

Trust - Legal arrangement where property is held by trustee for benefit of beneficiaries, useful for estate planning.

U

Urban Expansion - Growth of cities into surrounding areas, creating new investment opportunities in satellite communities.

Urbanization - Process of population migration from rural to urban areas, driving housing demand in cities.

V

Valuation - Professional assessment of property's market value, required for mortgages and insurance.

Vendor - Legal term for property seller in a transaction.

Verification - Process of confirming accuracy and authenticity of documents, claims, or property conditions.

Y

Yield - Return on investment, expressed as annual percentage of initial investment amount.

Z

Zoning - Government designation of land use (residential, commercial, industrial) that affects development possibilities and property values.

INDEX

9 781764 314916